To Hari and Daria

Hope you enjoy reading
this

x x

Joanna

When Mr Putin Stole My Painting

Ten Short Stories

Joannah Yacoub

QUARTET

First published in 2015 by Quartet Books Limited
A member of the Namara Group
27 Goodge Street, London W1T 2LD
A catalogue record for this book
is available from the British Library
ISBN 978 0 7043 7397 6
Typeset by Josh Bryson
Printed and bound in Great Britain by
T J International Ltd, Padstow, Cornwall

CONTENTS

When Mr Putin Stole My Painting

Henry had finally reopened his gallery in Beirut. He'd been in the States for months and, to be honest, I went in to say hallo or *hamdulla-ala-salaamtak*, rather than to buy anything. He was sorting through canvases and heaving a despondent sigh at every one. When I looked over his shoulder, I could see why; awful orientalist kitsch with flabby odalisques, masticating camels and wonky pyramids. I noticed the officer but decided to ignore him.

'Not your usual selection, Henry,' I commented.

'I bought them during the fighting,' he said, scratching the web of veins around his nose. 'People were begging for cash and I must have succumbed to sympathy; most unlike me.'

Henry, a short plump man, lit another cigarette and flopped into the threadbare armchair by his desk. My eyes strayed involuntarily to the officer who was leaning against a battered Italianate sideboard. Again I looked away.

1

'I had a triple bypass in America, and a new aortic valve,' Henry said laconically. My raised eyebrows at the cigarette provoked a dismissive flap of his podgy hand. 'Nicotine kills germs,' he announced defiantly. 'Spray tobacco water over your roses and they'll never get bugs. It's completely natural, not like the commercial stuff.'

'An infested rose bush isn't quite the same as lungs or arteries,' I suggested tentatively. 'Did you have a heart attack?'

'I'd had a few twinges,' he admitted. 'The cardiologist asked if I exercised. I told him the very idea gave me palpitations.' Henry stubbed out the cigarette. 'I left the carpet seller next door in charge. He didn't shift a single item, though I'm not surprised. That's the only decent piece.' He gestured at the officer.

Picking up a chubby bronze cherub perched on a chipped marble plinth, I read *Galeries Lafayette, Boulevard Haussmann, Paris* on the label underneath.

'There's a collectors' fair at the Bristol next month,' Henry muttered, relieving me of the cherub. 'I'll unload this rubbish in the opening afternoon.' He gave a wry smile and lit another cigarette. 'People go crazy at these events. They come with their friends to outspend each other, but seriously,' he tipped his head towards the sideboard, 'he's a real charmer.'

'I steer clear of portraits, even ones with bright blue eyes,' I said. 'Fudging a pseudo heritage with other people's ancestors is pathetic. That's why I don't go to English country house sales: everyone fighting over third-rate paintings of fat squires and their hatchet-faced wives.'

'Who'll bid me two hundred for this superb all-purpose granny,' Henry chuckled, pointing to a hideous painting of an old Bedouin woman. He went towards the officer, his cigarette smoke hanging over his shoulders like a dirty cardigan. 'Don't dismiss him out of hand,' he said, holding the portrait to the light. 'He has a sympathetic face and probably agrees with every word you say.' A bout of coughing racked Henry's body.

I felt oddly guilty, and who was I to play the purist? Hadn't I bought antique furniture, having none to inherit? I approached the officer, admiring his unblemished complexion under the neatly trimmed chestnut hair. The wiring in Henry's gallery was dodgy to say the least and though the lights flickered on and off, I could see a sense of humour in the officer's face and such refined features, I thought, even delicate, though not foppish. His uniform, navy blue double-breasted jacket with red epaulettes, was plain but for the gold buttons. There was no insignia of rank.

'I don't think he's a local. Do you know anything about him?'

Henry shook his head, propped the portrait on his desk and settled into his battered chair, its upholstery wheezing under his weight. 'An elderly lady brought him in,' he began. 'That fool next door said she was Russian, but anyone with a pale skin is Russian to him. She was probably French. The painting's too old to be her husband, but a father, a grandfather…?'

France has left its mark on Lebanon. Our favourite restaurant was Le Cocteau and "thank you very much" in Lebanese Arabic was "*merci ktier*". Our apartment was on Rue Lyon; our local post office near Rue Jeanne d'Arc. Collège Protestant on Avenue Marie Curie was one of the best schools in Beirut and in La Concorde, you could buy Yves Saint Laurent and Dior even as car bombs exploded a few streets away. This officer lived in less hectic times, though conflict has never been far in the Levant.

'Perhaps he was part of Colonel Jacotin's surveying expedition,' I mused aloud, before explaining to a baffled Henry that Napoleon was the first to commission accurate cartography of the area. The little emperor had examined the fantasies masquerading as maps; their spouting sea monsters frolicking off a Cyprus larger than

England or the obsessively religious 'Footsteps of St Paul', never mind 'Migrations of the Israelites' and had realised that if he was to conquer the Middle East, he'd better know the lie of the land. Myths cut no ice with Napoleon, unless they were his.

'The uniform isn't Napoleonic,' Henry said, jabbing his stubby finger at the officer's chest. 'Bonaparte's bunch wore cutaway frock coats, not tunics. He's definitely end of the nineteenth century.'

'Egypt was teeming with French officers when the Suez Canal was built,' I said, 'and some of the Franco-Arab community decamped to Lebanon after Nasser, or he could be German.'

'Beirut was full of German officers when the Kaiser built the railways: Istanbul to Damascus, Baghdad to Berlin, Mosul, Aleppo.' Henry rattled off the destinations like a station master announcing departures. He squinted at the uniformed man. 'Though he's not one of those clowns with duelling scars down his cheeks.'

'So he might yet be a Russian,' I laughed. 'They got up to all sorts of shenanigans against the Sultans. One minute they were championing Orthodox Christians in Anatolia, next agitating for passage of the Tsar's warships through the Bosporus.'

'Devious bastards,' Henry observed sourly, 'and they haven't changed.'

'Beirut always had more spies than stray cats. Look at our lot,' I remarked. 'Don't you have the vendor's name on the receipt? That might be a start.'

'The carpet seller is also a butcher. Administration isn't his forte,' Henry complained and pulled a tattered ledger from under a stack of unframed prints. Leafing to the relevant entry, he read aloud: '"Man in uniform sold by *khityara ajnabiyeh*, old foreign woman". Nowadays you don't ask too many questions,' he continued. 'Some of the expats can't afford to return home, or even stay here.' He shrugged and sat down again. 'What I can tell you is that he refuses to leave my gallery for a cent less than four hundred dollars.' Henry extended both legs in an exaggerated stretch. 'God knows how I'm going to get him out,' he grumbled, running his hands through his hair.

'Henry,' I protested, tickled by the idea of a squatter painting, 'he's un-named, unframed, unsigned and without provenance. He could be anyone.' I rather liked the portrait but if I betrayed any enthusiasm, Henry would claim it to be an undiscovered Manet, or some such twaddle. Turning my back on the officer and walking towards the door, I offered two hundred dollars.

'Three hundred and fifty,' Henry countered, leaping from the chair in a squawk of springs to block my exit.

'Two hundred and twenty,' I shot back, sidestepping him.

'Three hundred,' Henry insisted, intercepting me again. 'The canvas alone is worth that.'

'He's eighteen inches by twenty,' I said, 'not a socking great Gainsborough and that canvas wouldn't cost ten dollars...two fifty, and I've been to the bank so I have cash.'

That brought a gleam to Henry's eyes, though he huffed and puffed while totting calculations on a scrap of paper. I knew I was offering too much, but removing the purse from my handbag clinched it.

'You're bankrupting me,' he groaned melodramatically, his gaze lingering on the notes protruding from my wallet.

I removed three one hundred dollar bills, though not the crisp greenbacks of popular film, for Beirut fluttered with forgeries and Uncle Sam had halted the delivery of new notes until the shambolic Lebanese government cracked down on local enterprise. That America proclaimed "In God We Trust" on their currency didn't convince the cynical Lebanese who scribbled your telephone number across the face to hunt you down if the note bounced at the bank. Indeed, looking well-travelled inspired a confidence lacking in the offer of a pristine bill, which usually elicited vigorous rubbing to see if the ink came off. Henry's hand closed around the grubby money without hesitation, and the painting was mine. Except Henry didn't have change, neither in dollars nor in Lebanese pounds.

He recorded the details of the sale in the ledger and that he owed me fifty dollars. 'Come tomorrow, collect the picture and we'll settle up,' he promised.

'I'll take it with me, if you don't mind,' I said, apprehensive at leaving both the money and the goods behind. Henry wouldn't renege on the deal but in Beirut, tomorrow was a world in which anything could happen and frequently did. He wrapped the painting and handed it over. 'You've got a bargain,' he lied, his hang-dog expression unable to conceal the triumph in his eyes. 'See you in the morning.'

I shook his hand and left. As I entered our apartment, I held the painting behind me as if sneaking in a too expensive dress, only to be accosted by my husband who unwrapped it before I could explain.

'What's that crook pushed on you this time?' he asked, holding the canvas at arm's length.

'Who the hell is he, and did Henry give you a bill of sale?'

I brandished the receipt adding, 'He's no idea about the artist or the subject, but the brushwork is beautiful. Henry owes me fifty dollars. I'll collect it tomorrow.'

'You'll return the painting tomorrow and collect three hundred dollars,' my husband growled. 'What if it's stolen? Suppose a guest asks why his grandpa is hanging on our wall? We'd have to hand it over on the spot. I've warned you to be careful. Henry would plead ignorance over the Mona Lisa.'

I gazed at my officer whose eyes pleaded, 'Don't return me to that dingy shop. I don't belong there.' Perhaps, but that didn't mean he belonged with me. My husband, realising he'd been a tad sharp, placated me.

'We'll go together,' he said, patting my hand with irritating condescension. 'I'll see what I can get out of Henry, or from that oaf next door. If I think it's safe, you can keep him but the slightest doubt and he goes back.'

Looting achieved heroic levels during the Lebanese Civil War. Militiamen trashed luxurious villas, scavenged bombed buildings or simply barged in and stole from under your frightened nose, making it clear they'd shoot at the slightest provocation and often did anyway. A fortnight previous, we'd been approached by a dealer offering a complete service of nineteenth-century hand-painted Sèvres porcelain for two hundred dollars with a bag of Christofle silver cutlery for another fifty. When my husband turfed him out, he shouted aggressively, 'You're stupid. I'll sell them in five minutes,' and he probably did.

Lebanon was a bordello. There was no police force worth mentioning and though the fighting was over, too many deals shunned the clear light of day. The availability of precious pieces at knock-down prices exerted irresistible temptation, for who doesn't like a bargain, though the ultimate cost could be paid in social embarrassment rather than currency. But, as the militias were defanged and the population disarmed, reconstruction began with the boundless optimism that only the Lebanese can muster. House-warming was always a lavish affair where, dressed in your best, diamonds in your ears, hair sprayed inches above your head, you teetered along with your gift to an apartment which would have provoked howls of envy in Manhattan.

We'd attended the re-opening of a magnificent penthouse with an unbroken view over the lush gardens of the American University. I'd noticed another guest examining three silk prayer rugs. Our host, a real carpet fancier, began extolling their quality until the guest tersely described an embroidered logo on the back of each. The rugs were turned over and their true ownership exposed. The awful silence was broken by the quickest recovery I've ever seen.

'They came to me by kismet,' our host declared. 'I had doubts, but now I understand that my destiny was to return them to their rightful owner, even though I paid...' A jab in the ribs from his wife's glossy fingernail brought him to a stuttering halt. He'd paid three thousand dollars for those old Persians but could hardly sell them back in the circumstances, nor was the owner inclined to negotiate. Graceful acquiescence was the only option. The rugs were rolled and set by the door to be tucked under the jubilant guest's arm upon departure after dinner.

Next morning, we walked the few streets to Henry's gallery to find it closed. We left for London and returned after three weeks to find it still closed. My husband's pursed lips said it all. I'd been rooked of fifty dollars over a painting which we wouldn't dare hang for fear of its being recognised. Then one morning, we were driving past the gallery and saw someone moving about inside. We went home, grabbed the portrait and returned to find the 'closed' sign still on the gallery door. Two young men were counting paintings as if taking inventory. I tapped on the glass. One of them opened and wished me good morning in an American accent.

'Is Henry in?' I enquired, rummaging in my handbag for the receipt. 'We'd like to ask more about this painting and…' Something in the young man's face stopped me mentioning the fifty dollars. Nothing had changed in the gallery. The ash tray was full of smelly dog ends, Henry's cigarettes and lighter beside it, and the ledger lay open on the desk, my purchase being the last entry. Henry's coffee pot and cup were in the same place, their contents dried to a mouldy crust.

'Henry was our uncle,' they said, almost in unison.

I asked, 'was?'

'He had a massive heart attack,' one of them said. 'The butcher found him. We flew over as there was no one else to arrange the funeral.'

Unmarried, Henry had lived an increasingly reclusive life as one by one his family left for safer places. Confirmed old bachelors in wartime Beirut had Johnny Walker and the Marlborough Cowboy as their best friends, but that friendship came at a price and Henry had finally paid it. The other man examined the portrait, checked

12

the ledger and said, 'You must have been the last person to see him alive. The butcher remembered you leaving. He bought in that picture...from some Russian woman.' Whether he'd read Henry's note about the fifty dollars wasn't clear and I was shy to raise it. We expressed our sorrow at their loss and backed hastily out of the shop.

'So we're lumbered with it,' my husband grizzled, glowering at my officer. 'Henry was always cute when it came to money.'

'I don't follow,' I said, secretly pleased I still had the portrait.

'He coughed it before he had to cough up,' was his uncharitable explanation.

'I find that in poor taste,' I remarked. 'We'll take it to London where I have just the place for him, and even if we never learn his name, he has a lovely face.'

Christie's were as baffled as I was. Surprisingly, they gave him more than a cursory glance, even trying to date the canvas and checking whether he was a fragment of a larger painting spliced into a backing cloth. He wasn't. 'It's unusual,' they said, 'to find such an accomplished work of art without a signature. The brushwork is exquisite and he looks so fresh, yet he's definitely nineteenth century. Perhaps he was kept in a private room, away from pipes and cigarettes.'

A nicotine fug accompanied Henry wherever he went but leaving that aside, I was chuffed that my officer was described as a 'work of art'. Sotheby's declared that not only was it a beautiful portrait but that he looked a jolly nice chap; someone you'd welcome as a friend. His uniform had the flavour of Saint Cyr which might make him French after all, though another colleague's opinion veered back to Russian.

'The Russian-Ottoman War in the eighteen seventies,' he informed us, 'brought the Russians into the Eastern Mediterranean. No idea what he'd fetch,' he added, giving me a regretful smile. 'Unless we have an attribution, he'll be difficult to sell. You've no idea of his history?'

'For all I know,' I replied, 'he could be Vladimir Putin's grandfather, though I don't think he has any tsarists lurking in his family tree and wouldn't admit to them if he had.' Putin was the first name that came into my head. He'd just been re-elected to a second term of office and the papers were full of it. When I bought the painting, I, like everyone else, had never heard of this obscure KGB officer, now the second most powerful man in the world.

Calling it a day, I took the number nine bus to Kensington, went directly to the framer in Thackeray Street, chose a distressed gilt frame which set off his colouring beautifully and hung my officer in the entrance hall. When visitors admired him, I'd reply, 'I haven't a clue who he is but he might be a relative of Mr Putin,' and they'd laugh. Ten years passed.

One night I was unusually restless, though we hadn't been anywhere more adventurous than our local Chinese. Hovering between drowsiness and nightmare, I woke with a start when I heard sounds from the entrance hall. Giving my husband so violent a shake he sat up with arms flailing, I leapt from the bed with a yell of, 'He's after my picture,' and hurtled barefooted along the corridor, my cursing husband blundering after me.

The fluorescence of the street lamp cast a pearly haze over the dark corridor. A shadowy figure stood before the officer's portrait. Even in that faint light, I recognised the heavy-lidded eyes over full lips in a pale-complexioned face. He was smartly dressed in a grey single-breasted suit, white shirt and a striped blue silk tie. As he moved to lift the portrait from the wall, I launched myself at Vladimir Putin, the President of Russia.

'He's mine now,' I shouted. 'You abandoned him in Beirut.'

Vladimir Putin made for the door but hadn't reckoned with me. In a leap, I was upon him, barring his path with an umbrella snatched from the stand. The space being too confined to swirl it over my head, I gripped it like a stave to block his exit and jumped at him. Instead of pinning him to the wall in a neck throttle, I slipped on the mat and crashed to the floor, then scrambled up and lurched at the door, smacking the brolly against the wood with a loud thwack. Putin the thief fled and I saved my officer.

'Imagine,' I bragged. 'I got the better of the President of Russia. He's a martial arts expert,' I added, by way of self-commendation.

My husband stared at me in stupefaction and touched my forehead to see if I was feverish. Finding it cool, he took away the umbrella, led me into the kitchen and poured me a glass of water.

'I told you the lobster with noodles was too spicy,' he said. 'Your brain's overheated.' He was looking anxiously through the windows to see if lights in the building had come on, my assault on the door having made a racket. Relieved that our neighbours slept on, he advised we return to bed and discuss it in the morning.

'What if he comes back?' I asked.

'It's 7.30 in Moscow,' my husband replied, glancing at the clock. 'He's probably taking his shower.'

A vision of Mr Putin with a lathered chin, wielding his razor with aplomb, then stepping into hot gushing water materialised before my eyes. Recent news coverage of his Siberian fishing trip had left no doubt that he was, politics aside, a fine figure of a man.

'Then how did he get here?' I asked.

'Beamed over,' my husband said, not having a better answer.

Every day I see my officer smiling at me in admiration of my courage. He's still in his original place near the front door and, as I always check that the chain's in place before sleeping, I know he's safe. I often think about Henry who died just as the good times returned to Beirut and for that I am truly sorry, but he was thrilled to sell this painting and, merchant that he was, popped off with money in his pocket.

That night, I pulled off a remarkable feat. Though I didn't have the chance to ask if the officer really was his grandfather, I saw off Vladimir Putin. World statesmen haven't done that and I'm proud of my achievement. Someone out there knows my officer and, one day, we'll learn who he is but until that day, I'll stick to my original story. If Vladimir wants to pop by, he's very welcome, though perhaps not at four in the morning.

LAST CHANCE

Alcohol ruined my life and hurt everyone around me. I'm mortified someone of my intelligence and education could have deluded herself for so long. Everything was under control as far as I was concerned and any suggestion to the contrary provoked a sharp response. An alcoholic stops drinking and says, 'I *can* stop, so I'm not an alcoholic.' Stopping isn't a problem. Not starting again is, especially when alcohol is in your DNA. Finally, I was forced to admit that my entire philosophy could have been summed up as liquid Cartesianism: *bibo ergo sum*. I drink, therefore I am.

I ignored the not-so-veiled comments from the girls, or the warning lift of John's eyebrows, followed by a reproachful look. To my then state of mind, other people, especially John's business contacts, never grasped it was just for fun. You couldn't get a good discussion going either. They had no opinions about anything, or none they were prepared to voice. His colleagues were such prudes too. What harm was there in a bit of light-hearted flirtation? Everyone did it. I'd have a little tease and they'd all go pink, look nervously at their wives and then at John, who'd give that silly smile of his. And they were always going home early because of the baby-sitter or some crack-of-dawn meeting next day. I'd be warming up and they'd be putting on their coats. John would go off to bed as soon as they were out of the door. The notion of a friendly nightcap with his wife never occurred to him. Of course by then, the nightcap wasn't friendly and equally by then, I was past seeing that. What a fool I was. If now I have to define an idiot, it will be someone who thinks everyone else is stupid, as I once did.

When John began to entertain his clients in restaurants, I was relieved. 'It's only the men, Lucy darling,' he'd say. 'They're not bringing their wives so there's no need for you to come. It's just boring business.'

Can you believe I accepted that at face value? Of course you can. Did I prefer snuggling down on the sofa with the telly on and good bottle of wine rather than going to some over-priced restaurant where you never got more than two drinks? Of course I did. Would you believe I couldn't connect my idea of fun with John's increasing reluctance to share any aspect of my life, or have me share his? Of course you would, as would anyone with half a brain.

Our relationship died. We had no common ground except our two daughters and when Millie went to boarding school at thirteen, at her request I admit, we started to lead separate lives. Actually, when Millie was accepted, John persuaded them to take our younger daughter Annabel into the junior section though that was normally non-boarding. Boarding for juniors was permitted only if there were extraordinary circumstances. 'There are,' he'd explained.

We'd be a family again in school holidays but I was glad when they were over. Summer vacations were especially difficult. He wanted to spend as much time with the girls as possible and have them 'get more out of the trip than just a suntan.' I hated sightseeing and left them to it. A holiday to me meant drinks by the pool or in the bar, though I was careful in public. Tourists have nothing better to do than gossip about other guests and I didn't want stray comments reaching John's ever-censorious ears. Frankly, I preferred to buy locally and then stretch out on the balcony. I'd stash the empties in the wardrobe. That way the discovery would be after our departure and who cares what cleaners think.

From time to time, something would trigger a furious row which had to be 'got over'. Snivelling promises to cut back were par for the course. John would insist on seeing the supermarket bills; checking for booze of course. I learned how to circumvent that by shifty visits to local off-licences. Or I'd persuade friends to pop in during the day, friends whom I didn't introduce to John. I built an alternative social life about which he knew nothing. They'd collect the necessary on the way and we'd settle up in cash so there were no tell-tale credit card debits. John's work took him away a lot and no one was any the wiser.

Sometimes, I'd resolve to pace myself. That would work for a while and, of course, I could always stop, as long as I knew where I could lay my hands on a bottle if I felt like a drink. 'Felt like', don't forget. I never 'needed' it.

I rejected the very idea of treatment. My drinking wasn't a problem. I didn't become foul-mouthed, or throw up in public, or fall over. Perhaps I was over-friendly, occasionally a little boisterous. At worst, I fell asleep. I held my drink remarkably well.

'But that is your problem.'

I was in our GP's surgery, sitting in front of him like a schoolgirl about to get a detention.

'Mrs Carter, your tolerance of alcohol is exceptional,' he said. 'Physically, you can drink a lot. Anyone else would by now be either a raving alcoholic, very ill, or dead. At the moment I'd categorise you as a non-raving alcoholic, but you're still an alcoholic.'

'My father was an alcoholic. I remember how he behaved. I'm not like him. You've no idea what a real alcoholic is like.'

Dr Jarma spread his hands on the desk as if asserting possession of it and tried again.

'There's no difference between a real alcoholic and a fake one. You have an alcohol-dependent behaviour pattern, whether you like it or not. Your husband has tolerated it, covered it up, scrimped to send the girls away from it to a good school and struggled to keep the family together. But this is crisis point. You must do something, or you're going to lose everything!'

I was furious. Whatever gave him the right to lecture me like that? Of course, he would have it in for me. I knew how his lot thought; one drink and you were on the road to perdition. His wife was probably draped from head to foot in an entire roll of cloth and locked in the house until he came home.

'I've never heard such piffle in all my life,' I retorted. 'Anyway, don't drinkers live longer, all those polyphenols or whatever they're called?'

'Only if taken in moderation! Moderation means two or three units a day. A unit is a glass, not a bottle.'

'But I wasn't drunk, was I.' I knew where he was taking this conversation, but he'd have to prove his case.

'Technically speaking no,' he said, after a pause, leafing through the report on his desk. 'You were just within the limit on the breathalyser. The blood tests were border-line. You were going to the supermarket when it happened. It was eight-thirty in the morning; school run time. You'd already had a drink, on top of what you had the night before. Had you been alcohol free, you might have seen her, but you weren't, and you didn't. Witnesses have testified you had time to stop.'

I glared resentfully out of the window. If it was anyone's fault, it was John's. His attitude was insufferable. He'd had a fit of disapproval the night before, locked the drinks cupboard and had taken the key with him. Otherwise I wouldn't have been driving at all.

'Mrs Carter, how do you see yourself?'

I ignored the question. Dr Jarma forged ahead undeterred.

'Are you a contented mother, a satisfied wife? Why didn't you qualify? My wife's a surgeon, cardio-thoracic.'

Bang goes the shrouded prisoner theory, I thought.

He tilted his head towards me in a manner I found patronizing. 'Why didn't you make more of your life?' he asked.

'I've done well enough,' I replied. If he's going to start with the 'wasted talent' argument, I thought, I'll walk out.

'Did your father's difficulties spoil things for you?'

How could he raise the subject of my father! My father devoted his life to medicine and at the first whiff of trouble the medical world turned its back.

'My father has nothing to do with this,' I snapped. Dr Jarma recoiled in his chair and raised his hands in a calming gesture as if to placate me. They were covered in dark curly hair, like a small bear.

'I think it has, Mrs Carter.'

'Do enlighten me.'

Even he couldn't miss the sarcasm. He frowned.

'My wife was his junior registrar. It was common knowledge that he saw life through the end of the whisky bottle but no one dared breathe a word. The rule was "never criticise, never accuse," so he continued operating when he was, quite frankly, incapable. When that little girl died, it couldn't be hidden anymore.'

25

'But he wasn't struck off,' I shouted.

'He wouldn't have got away with it today. We both know retirement was the safest option. He kept his pension and avoided an official enquiry; one of the perks of seniority, I suppose. The hospital paid damages and the matter was dropped. But it must have been hard on you and your mother. There was a lot of ugly talk.'

There was more than ugly talk. There were nasty phone calls from nurses, even patients. These women were so bitter and their accusations so preposterous, it was unbearable. Finally we moved. And if they thought he drank in London, they should have seen him in Diss. Down and out in the ditches of Norfolk, that's what happened and, as he slid under, so did we. He couldn't even get work as a locum. Things became tight financially and our standard of living was a far cry from the comfortable life we'd led before everything unravelled. I had gone to boarding school at my mother's insistence, though Daddy was always against it. That ended, and I came home to find my mother hitting the bottle as well. She wasn't there for either of us. It was a mess. They're both dead now. But he was a good man. Couldn't Jarma grasp that? What did he mean by 'getting away with it'? I had to set him right on this.

'My father was an alcoholic. He couldn't help himself. I blame my mother. She chose to become a drunk. She pulled the rug from under him when he was at his most vulnerable. She could have stopped.'

'As you can stop?'

Dr Jarma stared at me in bewilderment, before he pressed on.

'Don't you think your father's refusal to acknowledge his condition drove your mother to despair? He destroyed her and your family life, just as he wrecked his career. He was shameless, you know, preying on nurses, boasting about it. No woman in her right mind would risk being alone with him when scrubbing up. What happened was his fault. Why do you have to go down the same path?'

'My father was always attractive to women,' I said defensively. 'They chased him, not the other way round and that girl's death was an unforeseen complication. A child stepped in front of my car. It wasn't my fault.'

'Please, Mrs Carter. Deny whatever you like, but he was drunk in theatre and killed a child. Another little girl is fighting for her life because of your careless driving. Where is the difference?'

'There's no comparison,' I said.

'You made excuses for your father all your life and you're making the same excuses for yourself.

It's time to face the truth, and about everything. I suspect things happened that you can't bear to talk about to this day: things you blot out by drinking. Don't forget, we knew him too.'

How much did he know, I wondered? 'What happened in the past is done,' I mumbled. 'I won't rake up old stories to satisfy your curiosity. In fact, I find your obsession with my father morbid.'

'I'm trying to find a solution for you, Mrs Carter. I don't think you belong in prison. I've been asked to make a case in your favour, but you must help me.'

No one had mentioned prison. I wasn't so blind that I couldn't see my world falling apart, but prison? John had set out his position in clear terms. He'd do what he could to help me, but our marriage was now on trial as evidently I might be. He wasn't going to let me ruin his life, as my father had ruined ours.

'You've caused a lot of grief, especially to our daughters, and they come first,' he'd said bitterly. 'Your mother took her own way out. I'll never do that.'

John's words were harsh, but he had a point. My mother committed suicide. I'd been up for the funeral but returned to London to continue my training. It was winter. Father had been drinking and was staggering home when he slipped on the ice. He didn't hurt himself, but was too drunk to get up and fell asleep by the roadside. He froze to death five minutes from his own home. The post-mortem revealed he'd have been dead within weeks anyway. His liver was so damaged by alcohol he was on the point of total collapse.

When I identified him at the hospital, a wave of guilt washed over me. My mother had had no right abandoning him like that when he was sick, and now I'd done the same. I wasn't there to bring him to warmth and safety. He always said he loved me most, and that what he did was because he loved me so much. I'd let him down.

Under the guise of needing time to sort out the financial situation, I gave up medical school and returned to Norfolk. It was a relief. The news of his death had spread like wildfire through the medical community. All the old stories resurfaced and though nothing was said to my face, I heard the whispers behind my back. To tide me over, I found a job teaching biology in a local school. It was ghastly, but I needed the money as there wasn't a penny left from my parents' estate, even after the house was sold.

When John came along, I grabbed him. He was a successful business man but, in private, had a mild and accommodating personality. My parents had hated each other. Those screaming rows, a kind of parallel yelling where neither listened to the other, had no place in my new world. John accepted that my past was a taboo subject and seemed happy at first to be always mopping up. We laughed off my peccadilloes while under the influence and, in many ways, he became an emotional blotting paper, absorbing, unchallenging. Even with sex, he wasn't the demanding type.

But John had no intention of being the sacrificial lamb in our marriage. He was determined to 'salvage something'. That's how he put it. I'd wrecked everything and even if I did sober up, there were no guarantees I'd stay that way. He'd tried enough, and he'd had enough.

Was I that bad?

I was. Though she was badly hurt, the little girl didn't die, so I avoided a manslaughter charge by the skin of my teeth. I'm not in prison but I might as well be. It's a residential programme and I've learned a lot. I had to. Booze wasn't my only demon. It wasn't just that I hadn't been there that cold Norfolk night when Daddy froze to death.

My mother's suicide was my real distress. I'd transferred all my suppressed anger onto to her because making her responsible for the catastrophe which engulfed us was less painful than telling the truth. Mummy had finally found out what had been happening and couldn't bear it. She was disgusted with him and above all with herself for not having recognised the signs. My obdurate silence was damning as within this unspoken world of horror, she saw how damaged I was and how in her pliant, self-effacing way, she'd failed me. She couldn't do anything about him, didn't know where to start with me and in her anguish, obliterated herself with drink and, at the end, barbiturates.

Jarma had suspected this all along and knew that unless I learned to articulate this, I would always be tortured by the memory of what should never have been. He's been wonderful and, with the team here, has managed to explain to my confused family why I'd used hero-worship as a perverse defence against the unspeakable.

The girls have adopted a 'wait and see' attitude, and they have visited but my marriage is over. There was no point being difficult, though my solicitor wanted me to press for more support. I've had more support from John, I told him, than I deserved. The time had come to give him back his life, so our divorce went through uncontested. John has already re-married so, yes, the conclusion is also obvious; all those trips and dinners with the men. I don't blame him, nor do I begrudge him the happiness I hope he's found.

When I come out, I'll be on my own. It's what I'd always wanted but now I've got it, I'm terrified. I have one last chance to pull my life together. If I can repair the relationship with my daughters, I'll be content. I'm no longer ashamed about what happened to me. My father was a bully who inflicted a travesty of love on a defenceless child for his own gratification. I am ashamed I destroyed a good marriage to a nice man and caused my own children such unhappiness. I put a little girl in hospital for months and her parents through agony as they sat by her bedside wondering if she'd ever walk again. Above all, I'm ashamed I threw away a promising career to live a lie, rather than face the truth.

I was under pressure to go into counselling; as a job, that is. It's understandable. I've had nothing but counselling in the last year so I know the tactics from start to finish. In my opinion, I'd be dangerous. It's still too close and who knows if I'm really cured. Being out there on my own will be the test. Not drinking is one thing. Learning to be honest with myself and others is harder. Slyness is second nature to an alcoholic and out of that grows manipulation, a lifetime of which is hard to shake off. So, counselling's out.

Instead, I'll retrain as an adult literacy teacher. As I relearn the ABCs of normal life, I can teach the same to those who fell through the system. I might even be quite good at it. Many of the classes are in the evening, which will keep me out of mischief during those critical hours and I'll have to open my mind to others, think about their needs instead of expecting everyone to look after me. The programme starts next week and I am apprehensive but I'm determined to succeed. I owe it to myself and it really is my last chance.

THE PAINTER ON THE
ROAD TO TARASCON

I'd taken leave of my battalion, and of my senses. Desertion meant the firing squad but I didn't give a damn. We were defeated. Our commanders knew it. The men knew it. Our terrified, homeless population knew it. Everyone knew it except those *Arschlöcher* in Berlin, who were deploying armies, divisions, brigades as if it was still 1939. If the High Command had bid *auf Wiedersehen* to their sanity, we hadn't. We'd fought our way out of France to make the definitive stand on our home territory. There we'd have the advantage, they said. What advantage?

Enlightenment began at Saarbrücken. As we raced eastwards through fire-gutted towns, seeing our citizens made refugees in the rubble of our land, we cursed the English but were soon cursing our leaders as well. We'd heard about the raids, though censorship kept us in the dark as to their scale but they couldn't censor a population and once across the border, we learned the truth. Minimal damage, the senior staff insisted, disregarding the incredulous expressions on our faces.

Our glorious collective suicide was to be the defence of Berlin. The Russians were less than a hundred kilometres from the city. We'd hurtled through the Ruhr at such speed we were disorientated. That was deliberate. Had we had time to think, we might have mutinied. We'd regrouped with another division near Kassel but were kept on base. Everyone knew why. Kassel had been flattened. Seeing that would have sapped our will to win, so they kept us busy with futile marching drills, tank repairs and so-called housekeeping. Darning socks became a patriotic duty.

We arrived at Magdeburg in the late afternoon. Magdeburg… My home town… Darkness was falling and headlamps were forbidden as enemy planes were harassing troops moving towards Berlin. We were to sleep in our vehicles. I'd nodded off, but was woken by Corporal Vogel turning restlessly in the cramped space of the tank. '*Mir ist scheiss kalt,*' I grumbled and tucked my sleeping-bag tighter round me, then realised I needed to pee. The cold always did that to me. I opened the hatch and saw snow sparkling like quartz under a sky peppered with stars. Rime-crusted trees shimmered under the moonlight and in the distance the twin towers of Magdeburg Cathedral loomed black against the indigo sky. I put on my greatcoat and searched my kitbag for cigarettes. They were right at the bottom so I hoisted it out with me, closed the hatch and then jumped to the ground. I relieved myself before lighting up. It was ten o'clock.

'*Wer ist da?*' the voice came. I held up the cigarette tin without answering. The sentry saluted me and continued his rounds. Our tank was at the edge of the bivouac. Before I knew it, I was crunching through the snow, walking towards those two towers beyond the woods where I'd played as a child, praying the railway bridge over the Elbe had survived, expecting at any minute the shouted warning, the click of safety catches, the shots and had they killed me there and then, I wouldn't have cared.

The Elbe runs swiftly under its smooth surface. I'd swum it as a boy and had learned not to resist the current but to let it carry me. Our favourite game was crossing the bridge on the under-structure, especially when a train was approaching. You'd be balancing on the struts, then hear that hum, feel the vibration, and then the shaking and ear-splitting din of hundreds of tons of metal thundering over your head. That's why I knew about swimming because I'd lost my grip and fallen in more than once. It was also why tanks didn't bother me. The smelly heat and rattling racket of the engine reminded me of my boyhood.

The bridge was still standing. A ladder on the river bank was propped against its lowest girder. Ice glittered over the shallows, mapping out the fast-flowing central channel. There was no sign of a patrol. I pulled on my heat-resistant gauntlets. Tanks are steered by joysticks which become hotter as the tank gains speed. They can burn the skin off your hands, but now I needed gloves for another reason. The temperature of those girders was below zero. I didn't want to freeze to the metal, the only escape being to pull away quickly and leave my flesh behind. My lips were shrivelling inwards in the extreme cold. I pulled my scarf over my nose, cursed my stupidity in forgetting my cap, hitched my kit onto my back and scaled the ladder. The sensation as I stood on the girder was bizarre. Normally, when childhood haunts are revisited, their small size disappoints. I experienced the contrary. The opposite bank seemed ten times further away than I remembered but I couldn't turn back now. '*Geh mal, Franz,*' I encouraged myself. 'You can do it.' I looked at the ebony water splashing against the pylons, saw the frost-whitened girders, remembered the pause points and set off, holding the uprights for stability, fixing my eyes on the shadowy outlines of my city, closing my mind to everything except getting across. At the other side, I shimmied down a girder, stood for the first time in two years in Magdeburg and wept with relief.

The city was untouched. A shadowy cyclist pedalled along the path. I stood aside to give him passage and wished him '*guten Abend.*' He grunted an acknowledgement and cycled on. So, I realised, there was no curfew. I walked along the unlit streets, hearing snatches of music from shuttered bars and *Bierkeller*. No one gave me a second glance and in ten minutes I was knocking on my door.

'*Mein Gott, Franz, wie kommst du hierher?*'

I smothered my mother's question in my embrace. Her face was emaciated. I could feel her bones through the winter coat bundled around her. My youngest sister, Gudrun, flung herself into my arms in a flurry of sweaters, scarves and blankets. Hannelore, my brother's widow, hesitated in the kitchen doorway. In the light of the one paraffin lamp, she too was gaunt. Resentment oozed from her. Kurt had sent her a rambling letter about killings and ditches and quicklime before being shot in Ukraine. He was spared Stalingrad though not the scorn of the

Wehrmacht. The official notification accused him of wilfully disobeying orders, which cost Hannelore her pride and part of her pension. '*Du auch?*' she asked, meaning had I also refused my duty? I didn't answer but went upstairs and changed into my own clothes, putting on two pairs of socks and two cardigans against the damp chill of the unheated house.

We tried burning my uniform but couldn't get a blaze going, so I stuffed it up the chimney in the dining room. My mother was looking at me expectantly. I tried to tell her what I'd seen and why I'd left. She brushed that aside and asked, 'Have you brought anything?' I was astonished. Surely she didn't think that it was like the early days when soldiers stationed in Paris offered gifts of everything from perfume to mink coats. Gudrun touched my hand gently.

'She means food,' she explained as my mother closed her eyes and sank back in her chair. 'There are shortages, now that we've lost France.'

I apologised for arriving empty-handed and said, 'We left in a hurry. I didn't have time.'

Hannelore turned on the radio but found only crackle. Fiddling with the dials gave her the excuse to turn her back on me.

'How's work?' I asked Gudrun, trying to lighten the atmosphere.

'We're transferring the best paintings to the Neu-Stassfurt Salt Mines, in case they hit us too.' She paused. 'They've built a huge underground factory in the old workings: aircraft manufacture and steel processing.'

'Do they still have manpower for that?' I asked.

'It's late,' she said, without answering my question. 'I have to be at work by seven.'

She rose from her chair and left the room quickly. My mother remembered herself and went to make me something to eat. I stopped her.

'I'm tired,' I said, wished her and Hannelore goodnight and returned to my room, closing the door firmly enough for them to hear it. I sat at my old desk, bent forward and sniffed the pine. It had that resinous, feral scent of a forest tamed by polish. The photographs were where I'd placed them two years previously: me with my father to the left of my writing pad, Kurt to the right. My father died of tuberculosis in 1939, not long after Kurt had married Hannelore. Pappi hadn't liked her. 'She's dogmatic,' he'd said, 'and won't understand him.' Kurt had wanted to be an artist. He'd studied in Munich but had stopped painting when they became more powerful. I was an art historian and had written my doctorate on Vincent van Gogh. Kurt and I had joked about that.

'Van Gogh's Descent into Madness as shown in his Brush Style,' he'd laughed. 'Thank God you chose that aspect or you'd have been accused of supporting degenerate art as I was.' Kurt had protested the removal from Magdeburg Cathedral of Ernst Barlach's sublime memorial to the dead of the First World War. Its critics found it insufficiently triumphant, though how they equated defeat with triumphalism eluded me, especially as Barlach had fought and many of them hadn't. Barlach's distraught mourners had been spirited into hiding. I suspected Kurt to have been one of the spiriters, though he never admitted it.

My thesis was accepted. It proved their theories. Artists who depicted the blood and soil glory of Man and the Nation were physically, morally and psychologically healthy. The self-obsessed distorters of reality who refused to toe the representational line were sick and to be suppressed. I almost cried when the flames from the bonfire of degenerate art rose that day in front of the Louvre, though later I learned that the better pieces of *entartete Kunst* had found their way to Berlin and from there, onto the international market. The examining board took my words at their most simplistic face value and missed my underlying passion, for I loved van Gogh's paintings: the vigorous brush strokes, the sizzling colours, the exuberant trees, roiling skies, upstanding gleaming yellow cornfields and the vibrant flowers. Above all, I admired his honesty, his ability to paint his suffering into his self-portraits without compromise. Their misreading made me Doctor Franz Halberstein, though that's not my name today.

Kurt's photograph caused me pain. He was grinning at the camera, his eyes crinkling in the brilliant Provençal light, the grass behind him rippling as van Gogh would have painted it. In the spring of 1938 we'd made a research journey together to Arles and Tarascon, where Vincent had painted his most luminous works. All that beauty, all those painterly opportunities didn't free this disordered genius of his misery. Vincent left Arles minus an ear, in emotional chaos and was soon to die. Kurt's smile was fresh, boyish, his hair fluffing in the breeze winnowing through those idyllic meadows. He didn't smile once during the fortnight's leave we'd shared in the summer of '42. I had thought it was because he and Hannelore hadn't had a child, but it wasn't. He was relieved they were childless.

My father's family had lived in this house behind the cathedral for three generations. Far from being a comfort, that familiarity was a threat. Everyone knew I was in the army and that I shouldn't have been there. Hannelore worried me more. She was capable of denouncing me to rehabilitate herself after the disgrace of Kurt's death. By lunchtime, I knew I couldn't stay. Gudrun guessed.

'We're taking the last paintings to Neu-Stassfurt this afternoon. I could pass you off as a porter,' she suggested when Hannelore left the room for a moment.

That would get me out of Magdeburg and I could perhaps make my way towards Weimar. My mother took some of her savings from her box, pressing them secretly into my hand before Hannelore returned. I hurried to my room, collected my identity card, whatever cash I had, removed Kurt's photograph from its frame, slipped it into my jacket pocket and then, on impulse, grabbed my Mauser and spare ammunition from my kit. Pushing the Mauser under the waistband of my trousers, I went downstairs.

'I'll treat you all to *Wirtschaft Krumm* for dinner,' I said cheerfully, and kissed Mutti. She clung to me, knowing she might not see me for a long time, if ever again.

'*Ich freue mich darauf,*' she said in a cracked voice, her hands twisting in her apron, her face blanching.

At the Kaiser-Friedrich Museum, Gudrun found me a porter's coat and cap to wear over my clothes. The paintings were already wrapped and, with two other men, I loaded them onto an open-backed truck. One canvas was leaning against the wall. I recognised the artist at once though I'd never seen this image of him. The caption on the frame read, 'The Painter on the Road to Tarascon.' It was dated 1888, two years before he shot himself, 50 years before Kurt and I went.

'You've forgotten this,' I shouted to Gudrun.

'It's to stay,' she said. 'The supervisor thinks it's rubbish, an unfinished van Gogh of poor quality.'

'It's the only one they didn't nick. Been here for years, but down in the storeroom,' one of the other porters chuckled and pointed at those in the truck. 'They're all stolen from someone, somewhere,' he said, 'and every detail properly catalogued. No reason to deny it. Owners won't be claiming them back.' He gave a cynical laugh. 'Ashes, most of them.'

That last sentence made me uncomfortable. I climbed into the truck beside Gudrun and the driver. We drove for forty minutes until we stopped by enormous double doors built into the hillside. The guards checked our papers, opened the doors and waved us into the mountain. In the enclosed space, the noise of heavy machinery was deafening. We were on a beaten earth road lit by powerful lamps suspended from the roof of a tunnel at least ten metres high and wide enough for three trucks to pass.

'They bring the plane sections out this way,' Gudrun told me. We passed a smelting plant, gasping at the overwhelming heat, as viscous molten metal was paddled along forming moulds by emaciated men using metal staves. Their heads were shaven. They wore no protective clothing. Many were barefooted. All were covered in scabs and welts, ulcers and great patches of raw skin. I was familiar with the labour programme. When it was introduced in France there was uproar. So many men of working age took to the hills, we had to rely on deportations to pick up the slack. I'd known conditions were tough, but I hadn't envisaged this.

'Are they foreign labourers?' I asked Gudrun, but quietly enough so as not to alert the driver.

'Some of them, some are Prisoners of War and others…are from Buchenwald. They built an extension camp outside the mine.'

Gudrun's tone was matter-of-fact, even nonchalant. She patted powder from her compact over her face and retouched her lipstick. We'd arrived at the art depository. A smartly-dressed captain, the SS badge gleaming against his *feldgrau* uniform, saluted her and courteously helped her down. He snapped his fingers. More skeletons in tatters, their eyes hollow behind sharp cheekbones, stepped forward to remove the paintings from the truck. They were so weak it took three of them to lift something I had loaded alone. I went to help them but Gudrun stopped me in time.

'Don't,' she hissed. 'He'll ask about you.'

'*Gnädiges Fräulein Halberstein*,' he said, bringing her hand to his lips in a formal kiss. 'Will you do me the honour of lunching with me tomorrow in Magdeburg?'

He spoke flirtatiously. Was there something between him and my sister?

'A pleasure,' Gudrun simpered. Their bodies were touching as they signed the paperwork. In her glance, I saw at once that they were lovers. Did she admire this kind of man? He symbolised everything my father and brother had hated. War had forced me into an accommodation with the system and I'd shut my eyes to many things his sort had done. That Gudrun had thrown away her purity for this *Schweinehund* was a betrayal.

'A new porter?' the officer asked, scrutinising me, his eyes suddenly suspicious. Had my revulsion shown?

'He's from the *Kulturministerium* in Berlin,' she replied quickly. 'He'll deliver the inventories.'

I clicked my heels and inclined my head in that precise manner favoured by the ministerial class. 'There was one last painting,' I said, ignoring Gudrun's horrified expression, 'a self-portrait by Van Gogh…set near Tarascon.'

'Not worth a pfennig,' he said tersely, 'to be burned.'

The paintings were disappearing one by one through a narrow opening into a side cavern. Tools, bricks and mortar lay on the ground. One of the wraiths began closing the entrance after the last of them had shuffled out. Snot was streaming from his nose. He had suppurating sties on both eyes and coughed a harsh barking cough. I registered the uncontrollable tremor throughout his body and knew he was burning with fever. He'd soon be dead and I could do nothing about it.

When the officer was supervising the bricking-up, I nipped Gudrun's arm and asked, 'Why?'

'He brings us food,' she mumbled, her face furtive. 'I told you, since France…'

'I shall return to Magdeburg with you,' the captain interrupted in a clipped voice, 'to inspect that Van Gogh again.'

I had no choice but to go with them. Had I not done so, I'd have signed Gudrun's death warrant, even if she was his mistress. They rode in the front with the driver. I shivered on the open back, frustrated at my lost opportunity to escape. The truck's cab had a narrow rear window through which I could see Gudrun and the captain laughing, exchanging cigarettes and jokes. He put his arm around her. She rested her head on his shoulder. Was she pretending affection to protect me? Should I have been so angry with her? The family had needs and wasn't he an officer, like me? Hadn't I followed orders, like him?

Though not yet five, it was dark when we arrived at the museum. Only the guard remained. I could hear a distant rumble, like thunder. We went to the painting. He lifted it from the floor, held it at arm's length and announced, '*schrecklich*! So crude and that stupid shadow, like a dirty coat trailed behind a tramp: good he shot himself for he couldn't paint.' Gudrun was giggling, perhaps from panic. The thunder was becoming louder. Still holding the painting, the captain opened a door from the gallery into a courtyard. 'I'm going to do art a favour,' he declared and produced a petrol lighter from his pocket and a vial of clear fluid from the pouch on his belt. Gudrun's laugh developed a coarse quality she'd never had. He poured the fluid over the painting, flicked open the lighter, sparked a flame and handed it to her. 'Your turn today,' he said. Her eyes sidled momentarily to me, but she accepted the lighter and approached Vincent. I could hardly breathe.

'I think you like this painting,' he said to me. 'Strange taste for someone in your position… Unless you are not that.' He smiled without warmth. 'Did you verify this man's papers?' he asked Gudrun.

Her eyes widened involuntarily. '*Natürlich*,' she stammered. He gripped her chin and twisted her face forcefully towards him. 'We will see,' he said and, swivelling on his heel to me, rapped '*Papiere*.'

That break in his attention as he pinched Gudrun's face was all I'd needed to draw the Mauser. I shot him without hesitation then slapped the still-burning lighter from Gudrun's hand. She crumpled beside his body, patting him, stroking his face.

'Why did you do that?' she whimpered, her voice thickening with tears. 'He was good to me.'

The list of paintings sent to Neu-Stassfurt was still on the desk. I added the Van Gogh, broke apart the frame, ripped the canvas from the wooden stretcher, rolled it, grabbed Gudrun's hand and dragged her from the museum. She resisted me, cursing me for a murderer and shrieked for help. The thunder had become a roar, a roar I recognised. A glow was rising in the south and when I looked up, the sky was dark with planes. They must have hit the salt mines on the way. The first bombs began falling on the factory area outside of Magdeburg. Anti-aircraft batteries boomed into action but the planes were too high. Gudrun was hitting me and screaming abuse, though her words were drowned in the mayhem which followed. She yanked herself free and ran. A massive blast blew me off my feet. When I came to, everything was burning. Choking in the heat, gagging in the swirling, reeking dust, I felt for the canvas inside my coat. It was still there, but Gudrun was gone. I saw her leg still in its shoe. Searching for the rest of her was pointless. A man's truncated body lay nearby. I found money in his pocket and his identity card, tossed mine into the flames and hobbled towards the Elbe before the mounting firestorm asphyxiated me.

That shadow, so scorned by Gudrun's captain, had been Vincent's sole companion. Gauguin had refused to visit him in Saint-Rémy asylum, leaving only money for his care and an untruthful message that he was going away. Forsaken by everyone, Vincent's turbulent life became a nightmare of delusion. Making him suffer such anguish again was anathema to me. I'd be the friend he hadn't had in Tarascon. Wherever I went, he'd go.

The howl of planes diving on a target spurred me to take cover. I ran to the river and crouched below the bank as they hurtled past. The shock waves from explosions and freezing water surging over me meant the bridge had gone. When I dared stand up, Magdeburg was burning. Only the cathedral remained untouched, its towers defiant above the billowing smoke. People were streaming from the town in a desperate attempt to escape the flames. Many were horribly burned, missing hands, hair, their skin blistering through shredded clothes. My teeth were chattering uncontrollably at the unbearable sight. Dishevelled policemen were herding this ghoulish throng to a safer point upstream. I went the other way, following the Elbe downstream as it flowed north to the sea beyond Hamburg.

My life changed on January 16, 1945. Unlike Kurt, I'd 'gone along', though I disliked them. As I trudged northwards, seeing what I saw, distressed that we had allowed those thugs to lead us by the nose into a war we should never have started, I accepted that the havoc wreaked upon us was self-inflicted but also, I knew that we too were victims. After 1918, we were a leaderless country, lurching from crisis to catastrophe, our families impoverished by the Weimar years until that man promised to make us great again. In our desperation, we'd believed him. Who wouldn't have? We became as delusional as Vincent and there were many who took his way out when the horror of defeat hit home. I soon had no money, no food and nowhere to stay except in Red Cross shelters or refugee camps. More than once, I pressed the Mauser to my temples but then I'd unroll the painting and look at that lonely man, tramping along a dusty road, laden with the tools of his profession and hesitate, fearful for his future without me. Later, even that changed, for though I'd saved him from the flames of Magdeburg, when I was climbing the gangplank of the ship carrying me to a new life in a distant country, I realised that having him had saved me.

'Nice painting,' the official in the immigration centre said as we awaited the decision.

'It's a copy,' I replied. 'My brother painted it when he was an art student. It's all I have left of him.' I showed him Kurt's photograph. He believed me and let us in

THE CAT'S TONGUE*

Such sport to burn a cat; my yowls sweeter to her than the tinkle of a palace harpsichord or a pageboy's piping flute. 'Slower, deeper,' she implores, squirming in pleasure, inhaling the aroma of blazing fur and scorching bones, savouring my agony as I'm lowered over the brazier, her silk-draped bosom panting over the tight-laced bodice, her pannier skirts shimmering in the flicker of the flames. She cackles as I scream, her Versailles elegance discarded like a whore's pantaloons when she calls her bet.

'Ten écus if its testicles burst,' she shrieks and, 'would that my husband had such a pair.'

I see the powdered wig, the slender arm stuffing money into my torturer's pocket, tickling where

---

* In the days of the Bourbons, a popular pastime for the ladies of the court of Versailles was to go to the main square in front of the palace, have a cat caught and then tied over a stick and burned to death in a brazier. They would lay bets on how long it would take to die and which parts would burn first.

she shouldn't tickle, giggling at his tumescence as I hang impotent, paws bound, skin sizzling, eyes bursting, spine arching and snapping in the flames. 'May death release me,' I beg as the spit raises before the *coup de grâce*, that last descent into the inferno and I turn to seal her painted face into my dying memory. She's forgotten the lives of cats and in my resurrection, I will know her.

Clothilde plumps the pillows and rumples the satin counterpane over the gilded bed. She sprinkles her mistress's perfume, a concoction of rose and lily with a hint of musk, over an exquisite lace chemise. 'The musk of cat,' Madame la Comtesse declares, 'stimulates the senses.'

'A splash of water would set her off,' Clothilde mutters, verifying that the bed is invitingly untidy, that the chemise lies as if it has just been shrugged off, that one satin slipper peeks from under the bed hangings, that the other is but a step away. She awaits her instructions.

'The ivory *robe de chambre*,' Madame la Comtesse Marie-Christine de Chatignac commands. She is sitting on the brocade-covered settle in front of her dressing table and is naked. Clothilde brings the robe from the cabinet and slips it around Marie-Christine's smooth shoulders, draping it behind her to reveal her rosy nipples in the milk-white breasts, the smooth downward swell of her belly to the triangle of blonde hair. She rolls up a silk stocking on Marie-Christine's leg, tying it above her dainty knee with a blue ribbon, the bow turned towards that place of pleasure, that place he will see when he unties it. Taking the silver-backed brush, she loosens Marie-Christine's glossy golden hair and brushes it down her back, past her waist until it flows into the folds of the silk, gold on ivory, shining hair upon shining silk.

The clock strikes five, heralding the hour of rendezvous. A pulsation trembles through Marie-Christine's lower lips. She snatches the hairbrush from Clothilde's hand and smacks her knuckles hard, revelling in her maid's cry, her limbs thrilling to Clothilde's pain.

'*Imbécile*,' she hisses, '*va t'en, salope*,' and pushes Clothilde towards the door. He will slip in, gasp at having surprised Marie-Christine *en déshabillée*, beg forgiveness for the intrusion even as his fingers search beneath the silk, caressing ever lower while his face nuzzles her throat and his tongue laps her ear.

Clothilde watches the corridor in case Monsieur le Comte appears but, sensibly, he does not. His wife is a favourite with the Queen which has advanced his position. Being a *mari complaisant* is profitable. The young Comtesse is said to be untouchable, but through the spy hole discovered in the side chamber, Clothilde sees that Marie-Christine is very touchable indeed. She is noting every trick her lover uses, every technique he employs, every nuance in the act and will put this to good use when she has her own *Maison de Plaisir*, for that is her ambition. Hers will be special, different, not only for the men. Clothilde will teach her boys well.

He is present, though Clothilde does not see him enter. Wondering if he slides beneath the door, she marvels at his golden amber eyes in a face too pointed, above a nose too snub to be handsome, yet he has a lissom grace. His unpowdered hair is glossy black and his garments, never removed, are sober yet costly, an intriguing diversion from the gaudy opulence of the palace. A wide, thin-lipped mouth curves generously, its perfect bow crowned by a fine black moustache against which tiny white teeth glisten. His tongue, flickering energetically forward, is richly pink.

'And richly effective,' Clothilde mutters as she watches it seek out Marie-Christine's creamy body, licking her throat, her titties and then her Venus mound, penetrating the soft curls around her slit, sucking up her clitoris as she moans and thrusts towards him in her passion. Having raised her to rapture, he crouches over her parted legs as if drinking her last drop of sweetness, lowers her to her bed and vanishes, despite her pleas for consummation.

The bell summons a gasping Clothilde, for what she witnesses excites her. She finds her mistress clutching herself in desperation, her face flushed and mouth agape in her craving for coition. Clothilde resents being the last resort, especially without reward, yet is grateful for the practice and has improved her skills immeasurably. She opens the cabinet and removes the *consolateur*, first warming it in her hand then, massaging her mistress's pubis to sustain the rippling response, she inserts it gently into the glistening vagina and strokes it back and forward until Marie-Christine's body bucks in satisfaction. 'I know that special spot,' she whispers to herself, 'better than any man.' Clothilde washes the ivory penis and replaces it in its casket, knowing she must now withdraw in silence as if she is blind, deaf and dumb.

'But not stupid,' she says after closing the door, 'for who is this secret man who creates such burning desire without tasting the joy so blatantly offered? And where does he go, for he is unseen in these halls?'

Clothilde dresses her mistress in a satin chemisette with silver-edged pearl buttons. She averts her eyes from the revelations of this shorter garment, knowing this is why her mistress has chosen it, thinking to herself that men prefer to unwrap it rather than have it on a plate. She will have no nakedness in her establishment but instead will offer the elation of 'unwrapping', she giggles to herself as she smoothes the stockings over Marie-Christine's knees, rolling them only so far to emphasise the brevity of the shirt.

'Make me ready,' Marie-Christine demands and presses her *cul* into the brocade of the seat, her eyes closing at the momentary sensation.

'Hotter than a bitch on heat,' Clothilde murmurs and glares at her mistress who slaps her face hard and hisses: 'Impudent girl. Who are you to stare at me? Do as you are told!'

Clothilde puts one arm round Marie-Christine and presses her to her own body to control her mistress's movements when her excitement mounts. With her forefingers, she strokes Marie-Christine's bud until it swells beneath her fingers and she begins to moan. Clothilde braces herself against Marie-Christine's spasms, feeling her moist heat and then stops. 'You are warmed enough for

him. Any more and your fire will die too soon.'
She hears the clock strike five and leaves.

This will be the last time she watches from
the side chamber. She has read her fate in her
mistress's eyes, knows that she will be soon
dismissed, her participation in such intimacy too
dangerous. She checks the wooden trunk into
which she has secreted sheets and pillowcases of
the finest linen, marred only by the scorch of an
iron or the munch of a moth. Three good silk
dresses are folded around lengths of satin and
velvet. Silver spoons nestle inside stockings and
a purse of purloined Louis d'Or golden coins
hides under a footman's velvet coat; all these
concealed by her second best uniform. When
she leaves, they will be invisible to the casual eye
of the guards and will provide an elegant start.
Clothilde has found the place, close enough to
the palace but secluded within its own garden.
She has already paid a deposit.

The door clicks on its latch. He is there. Clothilde
hears Marie-Christine's laughter, then a growling
sound and a yelp of pleasure. She rushes to the
spy hole and sees the chemisette on the floor, its
fabric torn, its buttons winking in the candlelight.
He kneels on the bed, Marie-Christine's thrashing
legs hoisted over his shoulders, his face buried in
her fork as his tongue rasps back and forward, in

and out with such vigour Clothilde can hear it. She presses her hands between her legs to quell her own response as her mistress propels herself into his mouth, sees Marie-Christine's belly unruly with sensation, watches her caress her own breasts in crazed delight. His hands are now cradling Marie-Christine's buttocks, scooping her upwards till her naked shuddering body floats towards his dark face, her hair a golden stream over the counterpane, her head rolling from side to side, blind to everything but the turmoil in her cunt.

'I beseech you. I beg you. Fill me, violate me,' Marie-Christine whimpers through contorted lips.

'What rot people talk when they're dying for it,' Clothilde sniggers, wondering if he'll be for hire.

'Burn me with your love. Make me blaze,' Marie-Christine wails.

Clothilde sees him pause, his mouth open, his tongue protruding as he smiles. He sheds his clothes to reveal a lean and muscular body covered in smooth dark hair. 'A panther of a man,' Clothilde whispers in admiration when his bright red penis bounces above his thighs as he positions himself for penetration. Deftly, he swivels Marie-Christine face down onto the bed, raises her parted cheeks towards the ceiling and plunges into her, his hirsute body flopping forward until he blankets her with his fur. He begins to roar and, as his act mounts to its climax, his voice rises to a yowling screech. Marie-Christine screams in passion, her slender white legs convulsing against him. But then, Clothilde sees them kicking frantically against his furry thighs, hears Marie-Christine's scream become piercing, her face no longer consumed by bliss but warped in anguish. She is helpless in his embrace and cannot escape the pounding hips, the energy so brutal Clothilde's arousal turns to fear.

He uncoils from his conquest and melts into the darkness of the room. The commotion has brought others running for no living thing ever made such sounds, 'except,' thinks Clothilde, 'a pig when the knife is sawn across its throat.' She follows them in and sees before her Marie-Christine writhing on her bed in a frenzy of agony and terror. Flames blaze from every orifice, her ears, her mouth, her nose, exploding in spurting tongues between her legs even as servants hurl buckets of water over her. Her hair becomes a fiery torch, her alabaster skin bubbles like pork crackling, her mouth gapes in a rictus of blackened gums as her melon breasts shrivel to burnt currants. Her bower of love is now her funeral pyre, the whoosh of flame all-consuming before dying inexplicably to nothing, leaving her a charred stump in the ashes of her bed. The rest of the room is untouched, the dark vestments of her lover scattered on the floor.

The debauchery of her mistress was well documented. '*Elle avait le feu aux fesses,*' Clothilde explains privately, 'and the fire in her thighs burned her,' though publicly she blames a fallen candlestick. The Comte, relieved the immolation did not burn down the palace, presses upon her a handsome gratuity and offers the dresses of his incinerated wife as a dowry for her life elsewhere. She accepts gladly, secreting the ivory *consolateur* into their folds, knowing how useful it will be when she receives her first clients. Her trunk loaded onto the post coach, she cradles the affectionate black cat she'd found crouched in the anteroom after the fire and, as the coach gathers speed, it licks her hand with its rough tongue, closes its golden amber eyes, curls into a contented ball and purrs itself to sleep in her lap.

THE BLUE DRESS

Purple bougainvillea rustles over ochre stones. Poplars, close as a kiss to the old house, sing in the breeze. Pale jasmine whispers scandalous tales of the blood red Damascus rose, its perfume so intense it clings to clothes, exposing betrayals, broken promises, infidelities on languid afternoons. Karima listens but never tells.

She remembers the dress shop, its silk damask curtains draped over lace-frothed windows. It was the most expensive in Beirut. A woman, her hands white-gloved like a doctor, had entered the fitting room carrying that dress. Mamma had slipped it on, smoothing the shimmering blue shantung over her hips, marvelling as the silk rippled like sea-water. Karima had promised not to breathe a word. Or something terrible would happen, Mamma had said, as she hid it under an old coat in the back of her wardrobe where Baba never looked.

School begins at eight. Karima counts her pencils, two black, one blue, one red and pushes her writing pad into the scuffed leather satchel. Her feet, tiny in white ankle socks with a blue lace frill, slip into Clarks T-bar brown leather sandals. She climbs onto a chair, lifts a floppy cotton hat from the hook, pulls it on and, hugging the satchel to her chest, walks along the cobbled lane between the houses. She pauses at the corner, turning to their house, searching out her mother's goodbye wave to carry it in her heart until she sees her again.

The school's water tank had burst that day. Karima was sent home early and found Mamma in the corridor by the sitting room they kept for guests. She was carrying a silver tray upon which was a glass of amber liquid rattling with ice cubes. Her hair, loosened from its bun, billowed in dark curls over her smooth shoulders. Her lips shone pink with lipstick and she was wearing that blue dress. Rose de Damas perfume scented the air and her cheeks were flushed. Dance music from the gramophone rang through the house, though no-one was dancing. There was no sign of Baba. He worked for Amo Amin, the wealthy merchant whose nearby house and garden were among the most beautiful in the city. Her mother had gripped her arm and pushed her into the kitchen.

'I'm expecting friends, lady friends.' Mamma's voice had been nervous, her body stiff and tense. 'You can't stay.'

'Why not?' Karima had asked. 'Is Aunty Mariam coming? Shirin's been sent home too. We'll play in my bedroom. I won't come down, I promise.'

'No,' Mamma had snapped. 'Go to Amo Amin's garden. You can play with the kittens.'

'Is Baba there?' Karima had asked, frightened by her mother's sharp voice, noticing another aroma. She heard someone use the telephone and then the click of the receiver being replaced.

Twisting her fingers in and out of the silk pleating which embraced her slender waist like an elaborately folded sash, Mamma had crouched in front of Karima and had gripped her shoulders. 'No,' she'd said, 'your father is taking Amo Amin's mother to their house in the mountains. He'll be home in the evening. Amo Amin will tell you when you can return and,' she'd given Karima a shake, 'remember, you didn't come home early and you didn't see this dress.'

The wrought iron gates of the Amin Palace had been open as if beckoning her inside. Two palm trees towered like guards of honour before the marble staircase to the closed front door. Cornflower blue eyes in triangular faces haloed in white fluff peered over the edge of the basket on the lower steps. Snowy paws followed, tentatively measuring the drop, then five kittens tumbled out one after the other and teetered on the edge of the step, unsure of their next move. Karima gathered them up and set them back into the basket. The housekeeper brought her cold lemonade and cake which she ate, before falling asleep on the sun-warmed step.

Amo Amin, smiling and handsome, had woken her. That same aroma she'd noticed in her house clung to him but she'd said nothing. After all, she'd promised. When she reached home, Mamma was wearing normal clothes and the gramophone was silent.

'Remember what I told you,' Mamma had warned, 'not a word, not even to your brothers.'

Karima's brothers vanished every day after school in a flurry of brown legs and baggy bathing suits before returning at five o'clock, their suntanned skins pearlescent with salt. She had loved to swim, darting like a fish between the rocks, her black hair streaming behind her as she'd plunged under the waves before surfacing in a burst of effervescence. Now Baba wouldn't let her swim. Grandma had said it wasn't right for a girl to reveal herself in public places.

'But she's nine,' Mamma had protested. 'She's a child. Your mother's hard on her, and times are changing.' Mamma had been angry with Baba for yielding on something he didn't believe in, but Baba respected his mother. 'Let's keep the peace,' he'd said, his palms upturned in apology. 'Karima can go her own way when she's older. It'll be a few more years.' Mamma no longer went swimming either.

Karima waits at the end of the lane. Taxis beep their horns, their drivers leaning towards her through the open window, but she closes her eyes and shakes her head, her pretty face wrinkling as she gestures dismissively at the hopeful cabbies. The greengrocer watches her. Her boundaries are the Amin mansion at the bottom of the road, still surrounded by its exquisite garden, and the overcrowded car park above them. Any further is forbidden. Karima knows the rules.

He gives her a Coca-Cola. She presses the cold can to her warm cheek, swinging in delight from side to side then holds the can towards him. He pulls the metal tab for her, waits as the carbonate hiss dies and inserts a straw. She sucks until she empties the drink with a funny, squelching noise then giggling, hands back the empty can. She returns home, running her hands along the wall, playing imaginary piano scales on the wind-pocked stones, unsure whether to continue.

If Baba has arrived early, like that other time, he'll become angry again and then her mother will make that choking noise. She'd watched his hand rise, saw the stick, heard the crack, heard Mamma's pleas as he'd struck again, saw blood spurt. She'd screamed as Mamma fell face-down on the stone-flagged floor, a dark stain spreading over her shoulders, past her waist and into the skirt of her dress, spoiling its silken sheen. She'd tried to shake Mamma awake, cringing at the blood-matted hair, the white jelly oozing through the shattered bone, when a hand had grabbed her, dragging her back, hurting her. She saw Baba's ashen face, his eyes red and swollen, his mouth slack.

'Mamma's best dress is getting dirty.'

'How do you know about this dress? Where did she get it, Karima?'

She'd looked again at Mamma, sprawled like a broken doll on the floor, seeing her grandfather's silver-topped walking stick splintered into pieces, knowing she'd broken her promise, understanding the terrible thing she'd caused.

'Did he buy it for her?'

Only the tick-tick of the needle in the groove of the record playing in the sitting room broke the silence. She'd stepped over the red puddle, crossed the hall, opened the door, recognised her mother's perfume and that other odour. Raising the stylus, she'd switched the control to "off", lifted the record from the turntable, replaced it into its sleeve, placed it in the cabinet and returned to the kitchen. Baba had slumped into a chair. Men in grey uniforms rapped on the door. She'd opened to them, hearing the squeak of the un-oiled hinge and watched the policeman force Baba's head forward, pull his arms behind his back and click the handcuffs around his unresisting wrists. She'd hoped he'd turn and smile as he was led away but he hadn't. Karima hadn't wanted to leave Mamma but another policeman had dragged her to a neighbour's house. Then Grandma had arrived and had slapped her face so hard, her nose had bled.

She peers along the lane. The house door is open, the kitchen empty except for Amira the housekeeper. The tiles are scrubbed clean and the blood washed from the walls. She sits at the table as Amira ladles soup into a small bowl and cuts bread. This is her favourite chair, the one with extra cushions. Without the cushions, she can't put her elbows on the table top although Grandma used to scold her, telling her it was impolite. Scolding had been Grandma's speciality. Karima was a deceitful little girl; that's what Grandma had said. Karima knows everything, Grandma had said. Mamma was wicked, and Karima was wicked for not having told what her mother did in the afternoons. Little girls weren't allowed to keep secrets, Grandma had insisted and until she told the truth, the truth which would pardon Baba, bring him from prison straight away, she couldn't go to school. Every day, she'd prepared her satchel and everyday Grandma had taken it from her. If she wanted it back, Grandma had said, she knew what she had to do. But Karima had vowed not to tell, so she'd stayed home, waving to her brothers as they'd left for school, then college, then work.

Three years after Baba left, a policeman came to the door, sweat seeping through his shabby uniform and staining a paper-wrapped package under his arm. Amira was hanging out washing and Grandma had gone to buy vegetables.

Karima, alone in the house, guessed the contents of the package and knew she must have it before Amira came in. She'd watched him, ready to snatch the parcel if he made the slightest move to go. Disconcerted by her unblinking stare, the policeman had thrust it into her hands, mumbling, 'Be a good girl and give this to your *Teta*. Tell her we found it in the storeroom.'

Clutching it tight, she'd run to her room. She still had the suitcase Baba had brought from a visit to France with Amo Amin. Amo Amin had bought it for Mamma as a treat, though Baba had been embarrassed by his generosity and had told his boss it wasn't necessary. Mamma had called it her weekend case and had promised it to Karima. Baba had laughed at Mamma for giving it such a silly name. 'Why call it that?' he'd asked. 'We never go anywhere for a weekend.'

Though Grandma had burned Mamma's clothes, smashed the dance records and torn up photographs, Karima had rescued a picture, the Xavier Cougat rumba record, the perfume bottle and Mamma's pink lipstick. Stuffing them into this black leather case, she'd hidden it in a corner of the attic where she knew Grandma wouldn't find it. Climbing to the attic that day, Karima had folded the dress and pressed it into the case. She'd draped that same moth-eaten coat over it and, as it had covered Mamma's blue dress, so it hid Karima's treasures.

When Baba did come home and told Grandma to go, he didn't mind if Karima put her elbows on the table, or if she ate rice with a spoon. Grandma had been wrong, he'd said, to stop her going to school. Grandma had had no right to punish her and Baba knew she wasn't to blame. What her mother had done was wrong, he'd said, and what he had done was worse. Did she want to try again, he'd asked. She'd shaken her head, knowing that everyone had grown bigger than her, seeing their stares, hearing their whispers. But to please him, she took her satchel every day, walked along the lane and then turned back.

Shadows under jutting cheekbones darkened Baba's thin face. A dusting of white stubble lay along his chin like thin snow on the mountain ridges above the city. Never without a cigarette clutched between yellowed fingers and in the evenings, a bottle of whisky on the table, he'd begged her not to become a woman like her mother, made her promise she'd always stay his good little girl. She'd nodded and tried to hold his hand to show him she was sorry. He'd pulled away, but had sworn to take care of her for ever. She hasn't seen him for a long time but she's kept her promise to him and, of course, to Mamma.

Now she sleeps in Mamma's room and keeps her treasures in the wardrobe. Today, as every day, she lifts the case onto the bed and clicks open the rusted fastenings. There's the record, cracked and unplayable. She runs her fingers round the grooves and imagines the music. A small bottle nestles in the silk of Mamma's dress, its label scuffed and faded. She pulls out the carved glass stopper and breathes in deeply. Only the faintest hint of rose remains but, to her, it's as beautiful as ever. She gathers the dress in her arms as tenderly as a mother lifts a sleeping child. The frayed silk, its stain an ugly black against the dulled blue, has become brittle, like parchment. Tracing her fingers over the delicate pleating, Karima resurrects Mamma's shape. She hugs the bodice, snuggling her face to Mamma's breast, feeling Mamma's slender limbs through the tattered cascade of the skirt, just like the time Mamma had tried to teach her to waltz. It had been naughty to hide it from Baba, but Mamma had loved her and Karima had betrayed her. She replaces the dress into the case, lays the perfume bottle in the curves of Mamma's figure and folds the fragile gown around it. There's the picture of Karima as a baby in her mother's arms with Baba behind them. He's smiling proudly and his arm is draped over Mamma's shoulder. She places the picture over the folded dress, closes the suitcase and returns it to the wardrobe.

She has another photograph by her bed, though she doesn't like this one as much. Her three brothers, those scrawny, sunburned boys, now fat and sleek with jowly faces, pose with their children. Such tall handsome men, they've grown up to be. But who is this wrinkled little woman with straggly grey hair sitting beside them? Karima doesn't recognise her and can't imagine why she's there.

THE VIOLENCE OF BEES

It's not our decision, but that's evacuation for you. We've been heaved onto a truck and shipped from the orange groves before we could recall our workers. They'll have a shock when they see the empty space. Not that they'll starve, but a roof over your head is important. Yesterday I smelled smoke and felt fire. Perhaps I should have sounded the alarm. We could have swarmed, but it's too late now.

The hive is hot. The truck lurches so badly, we're bumping against each other in a struggle to keep our footing. As panic mounts, my remaining workers are lunging at the roof in distress, their wings vibrating in an effort to keep cool. Below me, fretful nurses patch cracks in the larval cells, for this mayhem could kill our growing queens. A fluffy drone crashes into me and leaves me flat on my back, my legs waving in the air like a can-can dancer! 'You wait till winter eviction,' I snarl. 'I'll bite off your wings and kick you out, you useless lout.' Righting myself in the jolting truck is difficult but I succeed and voice a soothing purr to settle everyone. If I'm not mistaken, we're climbing, though God knows where to.

The drop in temperature is dramatic but we can cope with cold, though not with this idiot's driving. He clashes through the transmission as if dismembering it. Finally he stops and the engine falls silent. The tailgate drops in a clank of metal against metal. Footsteps clatter on the flatbed and we're lifted down. The ground must be rough underfoot, as we wobble before finding a level position. Birdsong penetrates our walls and I hear a breeze riffling through tall trees. I know their height without seeing them as I sense the creak of long branches and the slap of foliage against bark. Orange trees are closely bunched to protect blossoms and fruit, not sky-spreaders like these. The trap opens with a clack, flooding our home with the scent of herbs and conifers. I creep towards the light and peer out.

'Send the drones,' my second-in-command whispers. 'They're a waste of space, however much the queen fancies them and if they don't come back, hallelujah…fewer mouths to feed.' I'm tempted but I need to know what's out there, otherwise it defeats the purpose of a recce. It's always the same. If you want something done properly, you do it yourself. 'We'll come with you,' the younger workers offer. The hive has relaxed into a contented hum, and we won't be long.

We circumnavigate the hive several times to acclimatise and get our bearings. The air is fresher than on the coast. We're on a sheltered plateau at the edge of a forest of immense trees through which a path vanishes into their deep shade. Our first flight has the sun on our backs and I see the problem instantly. Jagged rocks protrude through ground slanting sharply from the tree line. The soil cover isn't even a spade's depth and other than coarse grass for goats, nothing luscious grows in our immediate vicinity. The wild thyme won't flower till next spring and apple trees on the hillside below bear only immature fruit and no blossom. My cohorts are circling me in alarm. On the coast, food was so abundant we've forgotten how to forage but now isn't the moment to reduce production if we're to survive winter.

Banking sharply, I lead everyone upwards to the trees, which I identify as cedars. They're the first I've ever seen but we're born with imprinted knowledge and I know what to do. The others eye them with trepidation, registering the dearth of nectar-laden flowers but, as I remind them, it's like the woodlands near our old home.

'Cedars, carobs, oaks, eucalyptus,' I intone, 'have the same harvesting system. Rather than tapping the source, we lift it second-hand.'

The juniors are perplexed. An experienced worker flies towards the trees and begins her sweep across the needles to demonstrate.

'Aphids in the cedar,' I keep it simple to prevent confusion, 'feed on the sap and secrete a substance called honeydew onto the leaves. We gather that and turn it into hive food.'

The worker returns, displays her full honey sac and that's all it takes. With an eager buzz, we plunge into the thick fur of needles, set our mandibles going and, tanked up, dash to the hive to trumpet the news. I note the sun is at forty five degrees to the horizon. It must be about three in the afternoon which gives us a good two hours to work. After such a journey, there's bound to be damage to the brood combs and the quicker they're repaired the better so, pushing my way through excited bees at the hive door, I begin my dance.

First I circle clockwise, then the other way, puffing out my belly to let them see and smell my honey sac. This tells everyone the source is close and what it is. I run in a straight line from the audience to convey its exact direction and position from the sun. The workers mimic my movements until they've memorised the route, transforming the hive into a melee of gyrating, scuttling bodies. With a flourish of my wings, I lead out a new troop, climbing in rotating flight until the cedars are below us. We ride the breeze, admiring the velvety green softening these craggy hills, then descend in spirals till we're on the leaf canopy. I'm about to join them in harvesting, when a movement catches my attention: something dark, smoothly gliding, not furry, not a bear, not on four legs, but I can't see two either. What is it?

I'm a poor flier in low light. Sunbeams dapple golden pools of luminescence across the moss-brown terrain between the trees. I dart from one to the next until I meet three figures filing along a track. The first, a male with two legs, carries those hoods and gloves our keepers wear. He's followed by another male on one proper leg plus a stick and who stumbles as he walks. The gliding shape is a female in a long dress. Her head is covered, leaving only her face and hands visible. She's pale, as if kept from the sun like our queen, and her eyes are cast down. Is she afraid?

They've reached our clearing where their leader carefully approaches our hive, talking and pointing, though he doesn't touch. A contingent of guard bees flies forth but, as he keeps his distance, they circle the hive in defensive formation. We rarely mount unprovoked attacks as stinging is suicidal for bees, though a regrettable necessity on occasions. I move closer. The woman is helping the male into his protection, pulling the netting over his face and tucking it into his jacket. To my horror, he pushes her away and flaps his arm at the guard bees, which promptly form an attack group. I'm alarmed. This queen will be stung if my troops misinterpret the situation. Far worse is the violence he's shown to her. Even if he rejects the white glove, or won't be steadied on his stick or have his net tucked in, he mustn't shove her like that. Queens inspire adoration, not the rambunctious thrust of the drone bully. I hear the growl of the worker party who'd sensed the threat, left their cedar needles and have massed for battle. The two-legged leader is gripping the stick male's free arm, stilling it at his side. I swoop between them and my bees, signalling that the quarrel isn't directed against us and that they must re-enter the hive immediately. I've a more pressing reason for those orders. I've detected smoke.

Most animals flee smoke. We fall asleep. When humans steal our honey, they anaesthetise us with smoke, rendering us docile and defenceless; a stupid reaction if ever, though now isn't the moment to analyse this evolutionary glitch. If the wind carries that smoke up here, we'll doze off so I sound the retreat, checking for stragglers, hovering until they're all in. The humans have also scented it and have moved to the edge of the plateau where the view over the town we left only this morning is good. What are they staring at? I take a look.

Sidon's orange and banana groves are shrouded in a turbulent black pall. Silver birds with pointed beaks dive at terrifying speeds through this filthy cloud then soar sparkling into the sky as fire explodes at earth level and the air reverberates with loud booms. She raises her hands to wipe away water running down her face, but it's the reaction of One-stick which amazes me. He tears off the hood, throws back his head, bellows at the sky then shakes his fist at those shining birds before crashing to the ground like a chopped tree. His companions leap to his aid but he pushes them away and pounds the ground with his knuckles. She clasps his hands to quell his pummelling, helps him up and places the stick under his arm. He lashes out at her, misses her face by a whisker then stomps awkwardly along the path into the woods. The leader comforts the queen and together they follow, pausing only to close the hatch to the hive. Panic-stricken, I race towards it. He spots me in time and says, 'in you go. We'll see you in the morning.'

'Indeed you will,' I mumble. I'll teach that drone a lesson, if it's the last sting I make. Violence to a queen…never!

He didn't need to close the trap yesterday, for we rarely venture out at night, and we're not pigeons. Those bird brains have to be cooped up until used to their new home or they'd fly back to where they'd come from. We hive to our queen and wouldn't dream of leaving her.

The morning sunshine whispers it's time to get to work. I hear a click and a scrape as the hatch slides against the wood. Squadron after squadron departs in dark curls, before dispersing against the azure sky. I wait till the hubbub subsides, then slip out. Ahead of me, the path snakes into the trees, circumventing rocky outcrops which snarl like monstrous fangs from the forest floor. Flying slowly, my body tucked into cruise position with my sting retracted, I'm following its twisting course when I see her resting against a boulder, gloves and hood on her lap. She's turning her face to the sun and I register an ugly mark across her face. That wasn't there yesterday, I mutter.

Staying just out of reach, I dart from side to side to catch her attention and then retreat to a clump of ferns. Flitting nonchalantly among the fronds, I try to look as if I've just happened along, for she'll never trust me if I scare her into a swat. She watches me through calm eyes. I edge closer, intuiting she's not afraid. She pulls on a glove and extends her hand in a gesture of invitation. Folding my wings over my back to signal my peaceful intent, I alight upon the white finger. She brings the glove towards her face and observes me. Raising my tail to display my stripes, I pirouette then sit on the white fabric. She laughs as she walks through the forest, holding me at arm's length. Clearings reveal traces of abandoned cultivation: crumbling terraces, broken vine frames, a rickety wheelbarrow. I see a tumbledown cottage, its windows blocked by cardboard. Moss sprouts on the roof and the faded paintwork is peeling.

One-stick, who's leaning against the truck, isn't like our bumbling drones who couldn't sting their way out of a paper bag. His truculent expression suggests an aggressive wasp-man, the sort who gives us bees a bad name. He's drumming his nails in impatience along the battered bonnet as his mouth opens with a shout. Startled, I shoot off her finger. He grabs the stick hooked over the truck door and hobbles towards her. She shrinks back as his hand rises but I zoom between them, then zigzag before his eyes to deflect his threatened attack. Climbing as high as I can, I dive-bomb him with the loudest buzz I've ever made, making him duck and slap at me, but I'm too fast. Then I hover near her shoulder, registering his disconcerted reaction with pride.

'You left without making my coffee,' he snaps, 'without even laying out my clothes. Do I need to teach you another lesson?'

So that blotch on her face is called a lesson.

'You were asleep,' she retorts. 'I'll make your coffee and you've found your clothes.' She points at his trousers, where one leg is tucked below the knee. 'The hive had to be opened.'

I detect a tremor in her voice. One-stick snorts through his nostrils like a horse. A child, his eyes dark pools in an unsmiling visage, sidles from the cottage and hugs the woman's legs as he buries his face in her clothes. Perhaps he saw last night's lesson too.

'Are those bees more important than me?' One-stick yells. 'We've left everything; our farm, our shop, to drag out our lives on your bloody mountain top. How can I earn a living up here?'

'More than you will down there!'

Yesterday's leader is climbing from a battered yellow van. Yellow is my favourite colour, evoking buttercups and marigolds, honeysuckle and hibiscus. He grasps her arm.

'Lina, say again you ran into the door and I swear on our mother's grave, I'll shake you till your teeth rattle.'

So he knows. Lina looks away, her hand ruffling the child's dark hair as the wind puffs against her dress, smoothing its soft fabric over her rounded belly. The leader turns to One-stick.

'That farm cost you your leg. We warned you there were mines but you wouldn't listen and now it'll be even worse. You were slouched in front of your father's shop, chain smoking, drinking.' One-stick's eyes drop. 'Yes drinking,' the man continues, pointing his finger at him, 'until no-one wanted to go near you, so you took your frustration on Lina.' One-stick's head jerks sharply, his eyes guilty in a defiant face, but Lina's brother hasn't finished. 'The farm was useless and the shop has closed, so what is there to lose. They're attacking anything that moves on the highway. Go back and you'll all be killed.'

Lina's hand is stroking her abdomen and she's crying. I vibrate my wings in sympathy. Her brother yanks a sheaf of papers from his jacket pocket.

'This was our mother's property. I've transferred the deeds to Lina. Get to work, make something of yourself and stop hitting my sister or I'll drive you back to your shitty shop and dump you there.' Angrily, he presses the papers into Lina's hand. I fly as close as I dare to admire their red wax seals and green ribbons.

'Those bees could teach you a lot,' he says to One-stick.

He's right. Strict rules govern the violence of bees. We don't fight inside our hive or quarrel with neighbouring hives. Bees don't sting other bees and we worship our queens. True, we turf out superfluous drones in autumn and occasionally we destroy a queen if she's sick, but that's rare. Violence is permitted only as a last-resort defence against non-bee attackers, and many of us die as a result.

'I've found you more hives,' her brother says. 'You'll need them if you're to make a go of it.'

One-stick steps towards the truck but is waved back.

'I'm not letting you drive again,' the brother says. 'You can't manage the clutch with a crutch.'

No wonder the driving was rough. The van disappears in a blur of yellow. Quelling the urge to follow the colour, I concentrate on these two people confronting each other. Lina's husband has lost his livelihood with his leg, hence he punishes her. That's clear even to a bee like me, though his logic is stupid. She wants to live in her own home and away from fighting of any kind, which is common sense. I fly a figure of eight within this hostile space, pausing midway, for I've caught a whiff of something special, something sweet but before I can begin my dance, she raises her face to her husband and, taking a deep breath, says 'we grew up here. It was beautiful.'

His face twists. 'Your mother ditched your father and came here. Is that what you're planning for me?'

'She left because my father hit her as you hit me, though,' Lina's eyes stray to the stick, 'his anger had less cause. Mamma didn't want my brothers to grow up watching their father beat their mother. Boys who see that do the same to their wives.' She gazes at her son, her implication clear. 'When Papa realised his mistake, it was too late to change anything. Before our coming child is born, you must learn his lesson or it will be too late for you too.'

She's warning him and he knows it. I'd better distract him before he does the wrong thing, so I fly in bravura loops, adjusting my buzz to create a dialogue as I whiz close to him, then to her.

'Look at this silly bee,' she says. 'It's been with me since I opened the hive. Do you think it's trying to tell us something?'

He scowls but I dance on undeterred, conjuring images of lustrous grapes clustering under knotty vines, repeating my mime until the boy wriggles from his mother's hand and follows me to the overblown damascene rose on its broken trellising, its perfume rich as the red of its petals. Snow-white jasmine flounces over tumbling stone walls and gnarled olive trees ripple in the breeze, their unripe fruit inky buttons against the silver shimmer of their leaves. I keep the best till last for One-stick is beginning to grasp the potential before his eyes. Only then do I describe a fruit so delicious, so purple-staining juicy, a fruit which fed the worms which secreted the silk which clothed emperors. Intrigued, they follow me across the neglected garden until I present them with…

'Mulberry trees,' he exclaims, 'with fruit as long as fingers. There's a market for these in Beirut.' He reaches up to nip berries from under the leafy branches, handing them to his wife and son. I buzz in relief as she lays her hand on his shoulder and whispers, 'try it, at least for this year,' and he nods, sheepishly.

Now a colony of twelve hives, we have danced the rose and jasmine dance, the mulberry dance and most importantly the cedar dance for it's that honey which has earned our family the most. They've painted the house, glazed the windows, pruned the neglected orchard and planted more fruit trees, keeping us busy at blossom time as it is us who transport the pollen from tree to tree without which no fruit would grow. I believe One-stick is happy for he smokes us gently to sleep, brushing away our workers without harming delicate wings when he collects our golden treasure. His anger has gone and their new girl chrysalis pleases him. Lina's face has been without lessons since that day, though I buzz the laws governing violence, just in case he forgets:

Bee on bee violence is taboo.
Hive to hive violence is forbidden.
Never attack without provocation.
Withdraw quickly to prevent loss of life.
Respect your queen.

He looks at me, cocks his ear to my song, and obeys.

SOPHIA AND
THE ANGELS

Dilapidated houses, their peeling stucco sickly in the yellow light of street lamps, cling to the perimeter of the deserted Berlin square as if begging forgiveness for their poverty. A beech tree towers above the neglected garden, the shadows of its bare branches dancing on the grey cobbles. I hold my little brother Thomas on my lap and wait on the bench opposite *Tanzcabaret Bloch*. My feet are numb and my stomach cramps with hunger as I watch the cabaret's flashing sign, counting the lurid green stars leaping from the champagne bottle, waiting for that fan of golden light, a whiff of cigarette smoke and rattle of music when the door opens.

It's nearly midnight and the wind is Arctic. Thomas shivers, though he's bundled in an old blanket scavenged from a street corner. *Eins, zwei, drei*: the fourth star lingers until the bottle rights itself to start again. Before we left home, I gave Thomas a cup of *Malzbier*, children's beer they call it, to make him sleepy and stop him bleating with cold.

Mutti doesn't care. I haven't the faintest idea when she might send food but if I'm not at the door, she'll feed it to the cats. 'Puss, puss, puss,' she'll whisper, too drunk to remember we're hungry but not too drunk to flatter men into buying champagne and caviar. Bloch calls her his best girl and Mutti likes the job so much, she even works hotels in the daytime for him. Otto, the doorman, says liking it is Agnes's problem. The others do it to feed their children. Mutti does it for clothes and make-up. She's young and wants to look pretty so that talent scouts will whisk her to a life of glamour, maybe even Hollywood. That's why she came to Berlin after Pappi was killed but I don't think it's working out; nor does Otto.

The door opens. Propping Thomas on the bench, I dash across. Otto hobbles out, his crutch tapping the pavement. Lost his leg in Flanders, he says, hates to think a piece of him is still there. Pappi was lost in Flanders too. Mutti visited his grave with Grandma and Grandpa, so at least we know where all of him is. My mother doesn't appear.

Tonight it's schnitzel, fried potatoes and mushy carrots. Everything cold, of course, and the schnitzel's half eaten, but it's that or nothing. I often steal from Mutti's purse to feed Thomas, especially since she started bringing home uncles from the *Tanzcabaret*. So far, she hasn't noticed. Otto produces a beer bottle filled with milk and hands me something wrapped in a napkin.

'It's apple cake,' he says, 'and Thomas needs milk. He's getting bandy legs.' He glances across the square, hearing Thomas's snivelling grow louder. 'He'll soon be as crippled as me.'

When our landlady said my mother didn't know how to feed her children, Mutti told her to shut her face. I feel like saying that to Otto, except he's right. Thomas's legs are bowed and I don't want him to be crippled. I wish we'd stayed on the farm with Grandma.

'The boss'll fire you if he catches you stealing one crumb, never mind a whole slice,' I say.

'The cook won't tell,' he replies. 'Your mother's smooching a new client who's spending like mad: too busy to come out.'

The cake smells of cinnamon, like Grandma's did. I carry the food across to Thomas who is pointing at the beech tree. He gabbles in toddler's talk, 'big bird', but it's only the moonlight shimmering through the branches. Behind me, the overgrown yew hedge rustles like an hundred newspapers being unfolded. Before I start on the food, I check that we really are alone. Last week a pack of stray dogs almost had us. If Otto hadn't set about them with his stick, we'd have been mauled. I was so frightened, I dropped the food so they got it anyway.

I shove pieces of meat into Thomas's mouth. He eats the mashed carrot and I make do with the fried potato. Otto waits by the open door for the plate, so I wedge the milk bottle in the corner of the bench and leave the cake beside it.

'Look at you,' he chuckles, 'all dressed up. Trying to make your mother jealous, are you? Soon you'll be the pretty one and at your age… be careful.'

He closes the door behind him, leaving me feeling stupid. Mutti begged these clothes from one of the dancers and honestly, who wears a spangled red net ballet skirt and a green velvet gypsy blouse in the street? I shortened the skirt but made a mess of it so it's up at the front and trails the ground behind and the top's too low, showing my titties if I move the wrong way. That makes the uncles stare and stick their hands down their pockets, fingering whatever's in there. It's not money, that's for sure, for their hands are always empty when they reappear. I'd give anything for some decent clothes.

Thomas has eaten the cake and spilled half the milk. 'Couldn't you have left me one bite?' I shout, shaking him so roughly he bursts into tears, but being angry at a three year old is pointless. I tip the bottle to his lips, making him drink, remembering Grandma's farm where I drank milk every day and ate eggs and cheese and home-made sausage and where the only music was the lowing of cows waiting by the gate at milking time, or the cluck and flutter of chickens as eggs were collected.

Mutti wasn't happy there. Living with Pappi's family was boring. 'No proper jobs, not like the city,' she'd told Grandma, who'd pointed out there was always work on a farm. Agnes had fancier ideas which didn't include tugging udders at five in the morning. She left me there, returning every month with money and presents. Grandma said nothing, but as she eyed Mutti's frocks and fur stoles, her face hardened. The visits became rarer, then stopped altogether until Mutti reappeared one day, her purse empty and her belly sticking out above stick-thin legs. Grandma brought Thomas into the world, announcing that was her last service to Agnes unless she did her bit, then we could all stay, or she should take her bastard and go. She could leave me, her only grandchild, but not a stranger's baby. We stayed until Mutti's flirting in a local bar became the talk of the village and Grandma threw her out. 'Go to Hell,' Grandma had yelled as Mutti bundled me into the taxi, ignoring my pleas to stay and slapping me into silence, for who else would look after Thomas when she was working.

The spilled milk shines white on the frozen earth. Thomas's eyes are dark-shadowed like the panda in my picture book. Hell can't be worse than this.

'Let the devil take us all; Mutti, her uncles, me…' I announce to the tree and jump as it trembles from roots to top, though Thomas doesn't stir and the wind has dropped. Hitching him onto my hip, I wrap the blanket around us and go home, praying the fire is still burning.

This afternoon I'd broken old crates into kindling. I pile them onto the embers in the grate, watching the orange flames tickle the wood when suddenly the fire explodes into a crackling blaze and the room resounds to a bizarre throbbing, like the wing beats of the wild swans on Grandma's pond. Thomas sleeps undisturbed, his narrow chest rising and falling as I cower under the blanket. I peek out but there's nothing. That faint glow in the corner is the reflection of the oil lamp.

The outside door bangs. I wake instantly, hearing the chink of dropped keys, the pop of a champagne cork and bump of furniture as Mutti moves chairs to dance to the radio. She's giggling, which means she's drunk and has been sniffing that powder which makes her eyes wild. The music is loud enough to wake the neighbours, though it doesn't muffle Mutti's squeals and the uncle's grunts as he does what he's come to do. I hug Thomas to me, scrunch shut my eyes and try to sleep.

Suddenly I'm awake. Light is flowing over me, though I've turned off the lamp and the fire has crumbled to ash. A shimmering column stands by the bed. Lacking anything to suggest a body, it bends slowly as if to take a closer look at us. Strangely, I don't feel threatened but, to be safe, make a vigorous sign of the cross. It disperses into opalescent vapour and vanishes through the ceiling in a whispery puff. My eyelids become heavy. I feel myself sinking down beside Thomas and then nothing.

A wad of banknotes is on the dresser. I peel off a few thousand Marks, this worthless money of a defeated land. Both Mutti and Thomas are still asleep. The baker once caught me stealing but instead of calling the police, told me to come in the afternoons when he'd give me the bread from the day before. Today I'll buy from him and might even treat us to a cake. I thumb through the money. It's more than I thought and will run to eggs and milk, maybe even *Bratwurst*.

She's waiting at the door when I return and she's not alone. He's handsome, but something about him unnerves me.

'So this is Sophia.' His voice is deep, even melodious.

Mutti's makeup can't disguise the puffiness under her eyes. I push past them into the hallway but she grabs my wrist, snatching the bag of groceries as she drags me back.

'Aren't you clever,' she coos, forcing a smile through her painted lips. 'You've brought us breakfast…mmm, lovely warm rolls,' then turning her back on him, hisses, 'he asked about you. Can't you see he's rich, you stupid girl? He's a prince.'

Is this the client Otto was talking about?

'He's promised me anything I want,' Mutti whispers. 'Do whatever he asks, do you hear?' She shoves me towards his outstretched hand. 'Prince Grigori,' she simpers, 'doesn't know the area. Perhaps you can show him around while I make breakfast for my darling Thomas.'

Darling Thomas indeed: I could kick her. Last week she tried to dump us in the orphanage but they refused as we still had a parent, albeit a useless one. Prince Grigori's gloveless hand is warm, though the morning is bitter. As we walk towards Alexanderplatz, I return the *guten Morgens* of our neighbours then realise that their greetings are to me alone. I look down and see my shadow in the wintry sunlight but not his. Panic-stricken, I struggle against his grip then see everybody staring at me. Can't they see him? We've reached *Tanzcabaret Bloch*, and sit together on the bench where a faint trace of Thomas's spilled milk still shimmers.

'Sophia, do you really want the Devil to whisk everyone away?' His face is radiant as he speaks.

'What do you want from me?' I ask crossly.

'It's what you want from me that matters,' he replies, flashing a brilliant smile; 'gold, jewels, power? Your mother wants diamonds, and money of course. Tell me your heart's desire, little Sophia.'

I examine him. Grey-flecked black hair sweeps upwards from a smooth forehead. He's taller and more handsome than Rudolph Valentino. If it was his money I stole, I'm already in trouble.

'You're not a prince,' I declare, racking my brains for a way out of this mess. 'Mutti's always bringing home men who aren't what they claim to be. I don't know anything about you; for instance, what's your real name?'

He laughs. 'I'll tell you about myself later but I am a prince,' he insists, 'though not of anywhere you'd know. As for my name, I have none and many. Some call me Beelzebub, others Iblis or the Dark Lord or Lucifer.'

'Why aren't you ugly?' I ask, for even I've heard of Lucifer and should be terrified, except I'm not. 'I've seen horrible pictures of you with horns and a forked tongue and a tail.'

'Look at it logically,' he replies with an exasperated sigh. 'Repulsiveness would be counter-productive. If I were monstrous, everyone would run from me, and they don't. People keep churning out the same ridiculous goaty men or winged ghouls puffing smoke from their ears without making the slightest effort to understand my role. Absolutely infuriating,' he says, shaking his head and then turns to me. 'Look, I don't have all day. What do you want?'

I don't want to seem greedy or frivolous. 'Maybe,' I suggest, 'a roast chicken.'

'I offer the world and you ask for a dead bird,' he says and stares into my eyes.

'I don't want the world,' I retort. 'I want food for Thomas. He hasn't enough to eat.'

A gust of wind blows leaves into my face. When I blink open my eyes he's gone, obviously unimpressed by my request. This devil thing's a load of hooey, I decide, and probably another of my mother's hallucinations from that white powder. I'm imagining things too, like yesterday's column of light. It's the life we're leading and a square meal would probably cure me. Mutti's going to be furious. When I return home empty-handed, she smacks me so hard I fall over.

'My big chance and you ask for food,' she screams, kicking at me. 'Idiot! Selfish bitch!'

'Thomas is starving, and so am I,' I shout, dodging the blows. 'Look how thin he is?'

'You'll pay for this,' she threatens, her eyes blazing. 'I'll get the money from my Prince and you can both go to Hell.' Mutti smears red lipstick over her mouth, puts on her coat and flounces from the house, her perfume lingering in the cold air as she slams the door behind her. She turns the key, locking us in.

The basket by the fireplace contains a roast chicken, hot, crispy fried potatoes and a big red apple. I have run through our three rooms ten times but we're alone and the outside door is still locked. The aroma is irresistible and, though my hands are shaking, I eat what's left when Thomas has had his fill. A chicken isn't too hefty a debt to pay off, however it got here, and Thomas looks satisfied for the first time in months.

The music wakes me. Thomas stirs in his sleep but doesn't wake. I feel Mutti's hand dragging me from the bed. Her face is pale and sweaty, her eyes glittering as she hauls me into the other room and pins me down on the sofa. Behind her, I see a man silhouetted in the light. His trousers are unbuttoned, his mouth slack and moist. I kick and flail at Mutti, but she laughs as he rips my nightgown and clambers on top of me, his flushed face brushing mine in a slobbery kiss. I spit at him and screech, 'leave me alone. I'd rather die.'

'And what will happen to Thomas?'

I recognise his voice, though no-one else heard him. Mutti's friend is putting his hand and something else where I'd rather he didn't. I don't have time

'Take me instead,' I shriek, 'but save Thomas.'

The man falls from the sofa and stumbles away retching. Mutti, swaying slightly, brandishes a wad of Deutschmarks in my face. 'I'm not giving this back,' she says. 'He likes girls young and not broken. If I have to tie you down, I will: time to earn your keep.'

I flee the room. Thomas is curled against the pillow, whimpering with fear. If being raped is my punishment for eating that chicken, it's not fair. We're on the third floor so escape through the window is a non-starter. Whatever happens tonight, I decide, wiping my tears with the back of my hand, Thomas and I will run away tomorrow. A chair scrapes across the floor next door, then laughter and the clink of glasses. I push a chest of drawers against the door. It might just hold them off.

A sound, like a breeze sighing through woodlands, whispers around me. Three columns of light appear in a swish of wings. If I squint, I can just make out a trace of feathers, a flow of robes like the carved angels on the cathedral walls, and they're as silent.

'Thank you for the chicken,' I say, remembering my manners.

'They didn't do that.' Lucifer, who must have sneaked in with them, is poking the fire nonchalantly with a long-handled metal fork. 'Roasting is my department, and that ruffian has made a terrible mess of your nightgown so put this on.' He hands me a silk nightgown glistening with seed pearls stitched in an exquisite pattern around the neck and cuffs. Thomas is deeply asleep.

'It's too fancy,' I reply, returning it. The angels rustle with irritation, though whether at me or at Lucifer isn't clear. I don't understand why the devil and three angels are together in my room, unless they're going to negotiate over me, in which case they've left it rather late. Mutti and her client are thumping on the door and that chest won't hold forever.

'I apologise for Mutti,' I tell the angels. 'She's easily dazzled. I'd run away but I'm afraid for Thomas. Promise to save him and,' I turn to Lucifer, 'you can have me.'

'Here's the problem,' Lucifer says, slipping the gown over my reluctant head, its perfumed silk tumbling over my body. 'Only willing sinners are mine. I can't accept noble sacrifices. That's outside my arrangement with God…and them.' He jerks his head towards the angels who snap their feathers in confirmation.

'How can you have an arrangement?' I ask, finding this very odd. 'You promised,' I'm playing for time by reminding him, 'to tell me about yourself.'

The door is reverberating to violent blows, the chest beginning to move. Lucifer looks to the angels who shrug.

'I was Heaven's most beautiful angel,' he begins. 'Michael, Raphael and Gabriel are made of air…' the columns nod… 'but I am primeval fire. Then God made man from earth and asked the angels to bow before his creation. I refused. Why should I, pure flame, kow-tow to dust? I had an inkling how this new creature might turn out and history's proven me right. Look at your mother and her friends. Not impressive, are they?'

One of the angels makes a gesture as if to say, 'Get on with it.'

'God was furious and banished me to Earth until Judgement Day. I alone can talk to humans and be seen.' Lucifer gives a wry smile. 'I'm not such a bad chap, you know.'

'But you drag people to Hell,' I wail.

'I don't drag anyone anywhere,' Lucifer says. 'I tempt. They accept, so my victims are never innocent. Your mother traded you for riches. I tempted you, but you refused. If I can't tempt you into evil, I can't have you. That's Angel's Law. We'll agree on Thomas, but you'll have to accept a slight change in lifestyle as part of the deal.'

Mutti's curses are getting ruder. My options are running out. Even if I escape, what kind of life can I give Thomas on the streets of Berlin? But I need a commitment to his future before I'll go along with this. 'Explain how you'll save Thomas,' I demand.

A glowing column floats to Lucifer, who interprets for the angel.

'Raphael's spotted a family whose son is dying, though they don't know that. That boy's fate is sealed but we'll substitute Thomas, make cosmetic alterations, straighten his legs,' the angel inclines to me as Lucifer speaks, 'and no-one will ever know the difference.'

'Is that a promise,' I ask, glaring at the angels who've regrouped into a luminescent cluster. They bow and spread their wings in a chime of music, like crystals colliding in the wind.

'Will it hurt?' I ask fearfully.

Lucifer shakes his head. He's our only hope, I realise, and clasp his outstretched hand.

The chest tips over as the door bursts open. Red-faced and sweating, shirt tails flapping, the ruffian staggers in, followed by Mutti whose dress gapes to expose her naked breasts. She's drinking champagne straight from the bottle and laughs at the revulsion in my face. The man grabs my hair, pushes me down, forces my legs apart despite my kicks and falls upon me like a slavering wolf. I remember screaming, then a loud crack and a blinding fiery flash.

Thomas went to Raphael's family, survived the horrors of the Nazis and became a renowned politician. The angels guarded him well. He amuses everyone with vivid recollections of a sister he doesn't have and felt compelled to call his own daughter Sophia. As she grows up, and looks more and more like me, he rationalises these memories as visits from someone he perhaps knew in another life.

Michael, Rafael and Gabriel are superior to me, but at least I'm not *schrecklich*, like Mr Rilke's angel. From time to time I bump into Lucifer and I confess to a soft spot for him. I've no regrets taking his hand, as a decent life wasn't on the cards for me. Thomas was given that, and the pleasure of watching my niece Sophia grow into a beautiful and talented young woman far outweighs the loss of what I was never going to have. I'm content.

BERLIN DAILY STAR, DECEMBER 18TH 1924: *Die Polizeitruppen were called to an apartment in the Herrenstrasse late last night following neighbours' reports of screaming, an explosion and a smell of burning. Breaking into the home of Agnes Kesselmeyer, a bar hostess, they found two bodies charred beyond recognition though nothing else in the room was burned. Police also discovered the body of her daughter Sophia who was wearing a pearl-embroidered silk nightgown and was untouched by fire. Her golden hair was spread across the floor and her hands were folded peacefully across her breast like a sleeping angel. Of her three year old brother Thomas, there was no*

sign. They locked the door behind them, leaving a policeman as security, but upon returning to collect the bodies, Sophia had vanished. All that remained was a spangled red net ballet skirt and a green velvet blouse which neighbours remembered her wearing earlier that day. Police are mystified.

The Dream Stealer

Cardboard boxes balanced precariously on Professor Jildani's desk. This disorder was alien to his nature. So was retirement, a notion he'd rejected for years until forced to concede the time had come. A former judge and Dean Emeritus of Istanbul University's Law Department, Hikmet Jildani was renowned for his encyclopaedic knowledge of legal events in modern Turkey and for his equally encyclopaedic archives. 'But look at it,' he muttered. 'Reference books, notes, reports…all catalogued but hardly ever used. I'm Turkey's most eminent squirrel.'

'How do you pack off a career of fifty years?' he'd asked his wife.

'You start with the first cabinet, then the next and so on until you've finished. After that, the drawers…'

Her advice was sensible but unhelpful, given the quantity of dossiers. The University offered a shredder but what should he shred, what should he save, what should he donate to the law school?

He'd qualified in the turbulent 1920's. The reactionary and incompetent sultans had allowed Turkey's once-glorious Ottoman Empire to crumble like stale cake left out for winter birds before Mustafa Kemal imposed his cataclysmic change upon the country. Hikmet remembered the deportations of Greeks to Greece and Turks from Greece back to Turkey; thousands of bewildered individuals from both sides of the Aegean being "returned" to an alien land, forsaking houses, livestock, and friends to wash up on unfamiliar shores where they had nothing. These population exchanges had always struck him as illogical, given that their purpose was to create a modern secular nation, 'not a one-religion state,' he said, recalling the chaos and the cruelty, 'and it didn't stop there. They at least survived.'

In the old days, law was administered by the Qadi, or religious judge; usually an official of the mosque, perhaps even the Imam himself. Ataturk's reforms swept this away in the blink of an eye. With serious crimes being referred to the larger cities, junior circuit judges, as Jildani then was, pronounced on feuds about water wells, vendettas over inherited scraps of barren land and accusations of curse-laying. Any illusions he may have harboured on the nature of "homo Turcus" were quickly stripped away. In these remote districts, Solomon himself would have been frustrated so how was he, a city boy from Istanbul, supposed to cope. Yet he wouldn't have missed a minute of it. He rifled through a stack of documents. A scuffed green portfolio bound with frayed red tapes lay at the bottom of the heap.

'So that's where you've been hiding,' he grumbled as he tugged it out and untied the tapes. Opening it, he leafed through its pages, recalling every detail of that day as if it were yesterday. This was a case he'd never forgotten.

The trial, if it could be called that, took place in 1929 in the little town of Urgup in Southern Turkey. Urgup had lovely old buildings, winding cobbled lanes, jasmine-scented arcades and a picturesque ruined castle. Sadly, many of its houses stood empty and forlorn, their Greek Orthodox owners having suffered the "repatriation" of their sect in the secular revolution. Urgup's courthouse, adjacent to the old mosque with its lop-sided minaret, was a pretty place tiled in blue and white Iznik and with a flowered courtyard.

The day had started badly. Their car had broken down three miles from Urgup forcing Jildani and Mehmet his Clerk of the Court, who also doubled as his driver, to walk the remaining distance. A hot wind blew from the surrounding arid peaks. Struggling under the weight of registers and statute books, they'd arrived late to find supplicants brandishing tattered papers and complaining loudly about the delay. Jildani's robes were sticking to his skin and he had a headache.

The opening case set the tone. A cow had been "lent" by one farmer to another. While in the borrower's possession, the cow had died. Compensation to the value of the live cow was demanded by the lender. The borrower insisted on paying the value of the dead cow. And therein lay the dispute between two disgruntled peasants. Mercifully the cow had died of her own free will, thus avoiding complications of culpability.

Jildani assessed the situation, though thankfully not the corpse which had been disposed of. Being old, her meat value was negligible though the hide and horns had to be considered. Her future breeding potential was a hypothesis rejected by the borrower as ridiculous in such an ancient cow. Jildani decided the borrower should provide the lender with a female calf and five bales of hay. After much slapping of hands on heads and tearful proclamations that they'd both been robbed, his verdict was accepted. The plaintiffs pressed their thumbs into the red wax seal on the official register and bowed formally to each other, thereby closing the case once and for all.

Mehmet stepped forward to announce the next petitioners. Glaring at a point high on the blue-tiled wall behind the bench, he shouted, 'plaintiff Azmi Hatim against Musa Hatim, defendant. Accusation against the said Musa; that he has stolen the dreams of Azmi, rendering him incapable of work.'

Jildani looked at Mehmet, who stared past him, deliberately Jildani decided. He then eyed the two old men, each wearing the baggy black trousers and loose white shirts of Turkish peasantry. Both were tall, slim and slightly stooped with the weather-beaten skin of those who'd worked a lifetime in the hot sun. Clean shaven except for luxuriant grey moustaches, they wore white crocheted skullcaps from which wisps of snowy hair escaped. Their resemblance to each other was remarkable.

He checked the register. It listed the same address for both, so they were related. Supporters jostled in the visitors' area, a sector demarcated by a chalk line drawn arbitrarily across the floor by Mehmet. Although a physical barrier was non-existent, its symbolic presence was respected and the visitors did not spill over. The murmur of voices had risen to an excited chatter.

'Silence in court,' Mehmet shouted and thumped his walking stick on the floor. 'Depositions will now be heard,' he announced and turned a vigilant eye on the audience.

Jildani cleared his throat and asked Azmi to declare his complaint. As the old man stepped forward, he saw the childlike expression within the wrinkled face, the milky unfocused eyes, the ugly scar across his forehead which distorted the shape of his skull and felt his heart sink. Azmi hesitated, chewing his lower lip as if overwhelmed by shyness. This could take all day, Jildani thought. He'd have to start the ball rolling himself.

'Mr Azmi, why don't you tell the court your full name, your age, date of birth and what you do for a living?'

'Everybody knows me here. I've lived in Urgup all my life. Anyway, you already know my name, or you wouldn't have called me by it.' Azmi's milky eyes settled on the judge.

A babble of voices from the spectators confirmed him to be Azmi, son of Mahmoud Hatim and that he was indeed known to all of them.

'You don't understand,' Jildani explained to Azmi. 'In a court of law, the plaintiff must identify himself for the record, otherwise the proceedings are invalid. So please can you give me your family name, your date of birth and your profession.'

'I'm Azmi and I was born a long time ago.'

Musa Hatim edged forward. 'Azmi was born in 1862, though I'm not sure of the exact date. He's sixty seven years old and used to work as a bricklayer. Our family name is Hatim.'

'With all due respect Mr Musa, you're the defendant. You're not permitted to identify your accuser. He must formally identify himself.'

'Formal, informal, whatever, this is Azmi. We grew up together. He's my nephew, although he's four years older than me. I was his father's youngest brother and he was the son of Mahmoud's first wife, my wife's aunt by marriage to her second cousin Kemal, who…'

'Fine, fine, that'll do. I accept your statement as proof of his identity.'

The recitation of a complicated family tree would have added at least half an hour to the hearing. Despite the irregularity, Jildani entered the details in the ledger, the pen slipping through his sweating fingers. 'And he's a bricklayer?' he asked.

'Correct,' Musa said through his bushy moustache, 'like me. That's our family trade.'

'His grandfather built the mosque…'

'…And this room.'

Voices rising from the crowd confirmed their credentials.

'Mahmoud, father of Azmi, built the village fountain…'

Mehmet brandished his stick in the dust-hazed air. 'Order, order,' he bellowed. 'This is a courtroom, not the bazaar. No-one may speak without permission from Judge Jildani.' He banged the stick on the table with such a crack, Jildani dropped his pen in fright, spattering the ledger with ink. Having forgotten the blotting paper in the car, he dabbed at the mess with the corner of his handkerchief, but the damage was done. Glowering at Mehmet, now presiding triumphantly over the intimidated room, he tried to regain control of events.

'Mr Azmi, please tell the Court in your own words, why you have brought this complaint against Mr Musa.'

'Musa and his sons won't let me work. They're jealous…and they cheat…charge for more bricks than they use, and they're slow.'

Musa rolled his eyes to the ceiling and slapped his hands together in frustration. Azmi continued undaunted.

'So Musa stole my dreaming paper. Without my paper, I can't see my dreams. I've hunted and hunted, but I can't find them anywhere. I know he's got them.'

His gaze wandered along the floor, up the walls, across the ceiling as if searching for the missing dreams, before returning to the bench where Jildani sat. Azmi hadn't finished.

'Without them, I can't work, so I want them back. You have to tell him.' Azmi tilted his head to one side in indignation. 'He's even threatened to steal other people's dreams if they offer me work. That's not fair. He has no right!'

'How long is it, Mr Azmi, since you last saw your dreams, or your dream paper?' Jildani asked gently. Dream stealing wasn't on the new statute book. It hadn't been on the old statute book either. Azmi pinched his lips in concentration and counted slowly on his fingers once and then again, just to be sure. Muffled sniggers rose from the courtroom.

'One year,' he answered.

Jildani, who'd expected worse, turned to the defendant. 'Mr Musa, can the Court hear your defence? Did you steal his dream papers? Have you threatened his potential clients with similar theft, if they employ him? This is a serious matter.'

From the corner of his eye, Jildani could see Mehmet's incredulous expression. Sniggers became loud laughter. He turned again to Musa.

'Well, Mr Musa, I'm waiting.'

Musa's face creased into a grin, then he guffawed. He slapped his workman's hands on his thighs and swivelled on his heels to the people in the courtroom, tapping his finger on his head in an unmistakeable gesture. Still laughing, he swung back to Jildani.

'Effendi, you don't believe this old fool, do you? Can't you see he's simple...not the full ticket, whatever you want to call it? And he's half blind.'

'None of which excuses your behaviour. If you have stolen your nephew's dream papers, you must return them at once.' He scowled at the defendant and continued. 'The ownership of a dream is absolute and the right to see one's dreams is essential to the human condition. Robbing someone of their dreams is therefore character assassination, and a very grave crime. If you have done this to Mr Azmi...slow-witted, half-blind...however you want to describe him, I will not take a lenient view. I will find in Mr Azmi's favour and, if necessary, imprison you for...' he racked his brain for a suitable offence, 'identity homicide and dream larceny.'

Musa's jaw dropped in astonishment. A hush fell over the courtroom. The weather vane creaked on the roof above and a pigeon gurgled on the open window ledge behind the judge's bench. Musa clasped his hands to his chest.

'I haven't stolen anything,' he said, his voice apologetic. 'Azmi scribbles from morning to night. They're doodles. I took those papers, nothing else.'

'And what about telling everyone you'll steal their dreams if they give me work,' Azmi challenged. 'You did that, didn't you? Go on, tell the truth!'

'No, I didn't.'

'Yes, you did. You know you did!'

'Don't be such a donkey, Azmi!'

'Call me names, now, huh? That's all the respect I get…?'

'Mr Azmi,' Jildani didn't want a fight inside the courtroom, 'it's better if I cross-examine. That's how it's done. I ask, you answer. Do you both understand that?'

Azmi and Musa nodded.

'Mr Musa, did you threaten to steal the dreams of Mr Azmi's potential clients?'

'Don't be ridiculous. You think I'm as crazy as he is? I said that so he'd stop pestering people for work.'

'But I want to work.' Azmi shuffled awkwardly towards Judge Jildani. 'I love to feel the bricks heavy in my hand, to see them settle into their rightful place, to feel them grow into something greater than just the earth from which they're baked. It doesn't matter what I build. It becomes part of God's world.'

'Judge Jildani,' Musa butted in. 'Azmi doesn't have to work. He's not strong, as you can see.

The family provides all his needs and we do it with love, so he's not a burden. But his eyesight's so poor, he can't lay a smooth line of bricks. People started to complain. Often we had to redo the work and at no charge.' Musa adjusted his crocheted cap. 'I didn't want to tell him his work wasn't good enough anymore. That's why I took the papers he calls his dreams. I haven't destroyed them, or damaged them in any way. Believe me, I wouldn't lie.'

Jildani studied the ledger and then the two old men. Beckoning Musa to the bench, he asked quietly, 'suppose you and your sons do the outside work, the work that shows? Let Azmi do the inside work, those bricks which will be plastered over. That way, you avoid complaints. He'll keep his dignity and will feel he can still earn his living. But please return his papers. They're important to him. What do you say?'

Musa nodded. Placing his right hand over his heart, he bowed in agreement. Jildani could see genuine affection in the old man's eyes and knew he had no desire to hurt his elderly nephew's feelings. He would obey the court's decision, of that he was sure. Judge Jildani then called Azmi to the bench.

'Mr Azmi, Mr Musa has accepted you are an excellent bricklayer. You will now have the privilege of working indoors. Thus you are spared the heat of summer and the cold of winter. Mr Musa promises not to threaten anyone with dream-stealing and will return all your dream papers, so you can see them as often as you like. Does that make you happy?'

Azmi's face lit up and with a wide toothless smile, he bent low and kissed Hikmet Jildani's hand.

'Before I declare your case closed, Mr Azmi, is there anything else?'

'Yes, Effendi, I haven't dreamt for a long time. I don't know if I still can. Is there anyone who'd help me?'

A short, portly man waved his hand and pushed his way from the back of the courtroom.

'And you are?' Jildani asked, pen poised to add the name to the register.

'Hanif Soleyman,' he replied. 'I'm the local doctor. Azmi and I have been friends since childhood.' He clasped Azmi's hand. 'He can come to my house whenever he wants. I'll help him dream again and I'll buy him new paper and pencils.'

Azmi put his arm around Doctor Soleyman and hugged him.

'Then I declare the case of Azmi versus Musa closed,' Jildani stated, thumped the gavel on the desk and nodded to Mehmet to announce the next dispute.

He chuckled as he leafed through the folder. Nowadays such a complaint wouldn't reach court, let alone receive a formal judgment. On his return to Istanbul and regaling his city friends with tales of trials in rural Turkey, they'd teased him over the dispute of Azmi versus Musa. Even his family accused him of becoming a coffee shop storyteller. The arrival of the portfolio many years later made them eat their words. He spread the pages over his desk. The corners were curled, the edges torn, the paper stained and foxed with age, but the pictures were still clear.

'There was a letter…' His fingers leafed through the papers. 'Found it…'

He turned towards the afternoon sun streaming through the window, held the discoloured script to the light and read it again.

Dear Professor Jildani,
While clearing my great-grandfather's house in Urgup, I stumbled across these drawings with a note in his handwriting to say they were to be delivered to you. He died many years ago, but with the war and families scattering about the world as we do nowadays, they were never sent.

Do you remember the case of Azmi the bricklayer? Azmi wanted you to have these when he died, as it was

you who restored them to him. You may not understand their significance. Let me explain.

My great-grandfather had a special love for Azmi.
Each cherished a great ambition. Azmi's was to be an
architect, and he'd completed the preliminary courses
to enter Istanbul University. So you must understand,
Azmi wasn't always as you saw him.

In the early 1880s, the Sultans embarked upon
their disastrous Balkan wars. My great-grandfather
was exempted the general mobilisation, as he'd started
his medical studies but Azmi had to go.

After qualifying, Doctor Suleyman served in the
army, then returned to Urgup to find that Azmi had
suffered grievous head injuries and was irrevocably
impaired. The handsome young soldier who had
marched proudly away in his gold-braided uniform
was now a child. Azmi the man had been destroyed,
but Azmi the artist survived. These drawings were his
only link to what he'd once hoped to be. Sadly, he lost
his sight completely at the end and died not long after
the onset of blindness, perhaps five years after your case.

Friends in Istanbul told me of your position at the
University and though Azmi's dream papers are forty
years late, I thought you might still like to see them.

Yours Sincerely…

The signature read Karem Soleyman, the
descendant of Hanif Soleyman who had volunteered
that day to help Azmi dream again. Jildani hadn't
grasped what Dr Soleyman meant until he received
the folio. Then it made sense. He spread the drawings

over his desk and looked again in admiration at the dream world of Azmi the bricklayer.

There were mosques, archaeological sites and monuments, drawings of palaces, of basilicas and shrines, of monasteries, of local villages, of yalis and houses yet to be built, landscapes, statues, pediments, columns, friezes. Every style of building was represented. Some were rough pencil sketchs, others faultless architectural details in fine ink and wash. In perfect perspective and many with indications of size and scale, these drawings were exquisite works of art, even by the most exacting standards.

More charming were Azmi's sketches of local life. There was Uncle Musa, trowel in hand, lining up a wall of bricks along peg-lines, his baggy black trousers shaded in intricate hatching against the sunlit lustre of the masonry. A laughing child, delicate in watercolour, pointed a podgy finger towards the artist. Azmi's saviour and benefactor, Hanif Soleyman, tubby and professional in a neat suit, medical bag in his hand and standing exactly as Jildani remembered him, was smiling, his eyes creased against the light, his face glowing with affection. They were all the more remarkable because Azmi's injuries had affected his eyesight and whatever vision had been left was later destroyed by cataracts. Jildani recited an old Turkish saying.

'When a bald man dies, everyone remembers what golden hair he had. When a blind man dies, they say what beautiful eyes he had.'

He'd never understood this saying, until he saw Azmi's drawings. Azmi's future died in the Balkans yet he never lost his vision of what might have been and, through those shattered eyes, had recreated his dreams. It was that fulfilment which, despite his devastating injuries, made him a complete human being.

He tied the folder's tapes. 'We live in a hard world of hard facts,' he said as he laid it on the pile marked "home", a place where he would soon be spending too much time, 'and my dreams are all behind me now.'

As the brown spots on his hands and the foxing on the folder dappled together in the sunlight, he reached for yet another heap of papers, knowing that if he didn't continue, he would never finish, never be ready to write his memoirs, and never be able to tell the world about Azmi the bricklayer from Urgup and his stolen dreams.

Silent Night

Night is the groan of wind through treetops, a soft thrum of staying-out-late cars and hum of urban machinery. It is the vixen's shout echoing through the square to warn off the hissing cat, footsteps on a deserted pavement, a baby crying. It's Rosemary, jamming her pram into the shop doorway and folding cartons into a makeshift shelter. Grumbling to herself, she arranges her dirty sleeping bag, her ragged cushion and sets out her reading: a discarded newspaper, a tattered book. Tonight she will eat fish and chips with tartar sauce, extra peas and hummus. The hummus is new, for Rosemary keeps strictly English, but Mr Ali has persuaded her to 'give it a try.' Ramadan Ali has wrapped the freshly-fried cod in extra layers of greaseproof 'for the keeping warm' and has provided paper napkins, knowing Rosemary has standards. He also knows she isn't destitute.

'She owns a house,' he informs Ibrahim Haidar, in his sing-song accent, 'in Chepstow Road and she's educated…was a teacher. There's family too. This is news to you, is it not?'

Mr Haidar, owner of the kebab shop and offended by Rosemary's rejection of his tabbouleh, is irritated by her acceptance of the hummus. As if a Pakistani knows how to make that, he thinks resentfully.

'All I know is that she shouts rude words,' retorts the fastidious Ibrahim, who will only serve Rosemary from the doorstep. '*Tuz, tuz, tuz*, every other minute. That's Arabic for you know where and,' he whispers, 'she sticks her fingers in it. I've seen her.'

'She is shouting tush tush tush,' Mr Ali explains patiently, regretting the finger, 'and these words are coming from William Shakespeare.'

'He's an Arab?' Ibrahim asks cynically, observing Rosemary's cardboard shack with distaste.

'He's a famous English writer,' Ramadan replies, puffing his cheeks in exasperation. 'Even an unbelieving Lebanese half-wit like you is knowing that. I am onto this because her nephew has told me, and he's at St Mary's.'

Her nephew also knows that Ramadan keeps her debit card in his safe, and that he has her pin, for it is Ramadan who withdraws her weekly cash, Rosemary being unwelcome in the bank and refusing to use the ATM.

'Never know who's watching,' she screeches in that raucous voice which drove her mother mad. At three in the morning, it's usually the night shift from the police station, who last winter put her in a cell when it dropped to minus five. 'For her own good,' the sergeant said, 'but she wouldn't stay. Knew her rights and out by four. God knows how she survives. She's skin and bones.'

Her mother, now that's another story...of a bad-tempered woman lumbered with an unwanted child from a wartime marriage which shouldn't have happened, except it had to if Doris wasn't to be shamed. He who did the decent thing conveniently died of D Day wounds, bequeathing a house, an army pension and his parents determined to see little Rosemary right. Doris, bolstered by the benefits of her situation, bullied the child, nipping her arm, knowing she'd get away with it. 'Tell anyone' she shouted into Rosemary's face, 'and I'll glue your gob together so you can't say another word.'

'You're hard on her,' Doris's sister Muriel said, worried by the child's silent sullenness, angered by her sister's harshness. 'Let me take her. I'll bring her back when they visit, if that's what worries you.'

That worked a treat, until Muriel let them all go to the children's matinee, an act of such normality no-one could have foreseen the consequences, for Rosemary had a secret life of adopted voices. She mimicked the neighbour's Geordie accent, the lilting intonations of her Irish schoolteacher, the nasality of the florist whose allergies made her sneeze all day. When cousins Freddy and Henry settled into the threadbare cinema seats with nine year old Rosemary between them and the white duck in the blue sailor jacket waddled across the screen, she listened, and getting it right first time, squawked,

'Oh boy, oh boy, oh boy.'

By the end of the cartoon, her quack was effortless, the plosives eliding into sibilants and tempered by every fricative available to human speech. Rosemary knew the technique. Those elocution lessons her grandmother had paid for were harnessed to this contrary purpose and Rosemary proved their value when she sang the National Anthem in Duck style, earning a clip on the ear from Aunty Muriel for being disrespectful to Her Majesty.

'She does it to annoy,' Doris complained as Rosemary replaced her usual grunt to her mother with a cheerful, 'Hiya Toots!'

'At least she's speaking to you,' Muriel replied, hesitantly outlining the importance of getting on the same wavelength until Doris told Muriel that the only wavelength she listened to was the BBC.

'I can't bear babble,' she said. 'That's why I hate kids. They never shut up, and I'll have her back at the end of term,' she added grimly. 'Her grandparents will cough up for private school and she won't pass the entrance exam if she wastes her time on this rubbish.'

'She'll need a clean blouse every day,' Muriel warned, 'and breakfast and dinner. She's not the dog,' she snapped, 'where you tip out the tin and walk away. Once past twelve, she'll sort herself out but till then she stays with me. Or I'll tell them what you're really like. We'll see their reaction when they hear the truth.'

'And the dog did nothing in the night-time,' I shriek, feeling memory seep through my skin like ringworm. I scrub with the nailbrush until the red shows wet enough to wipe.

I passed of course, though I tried not to. Don't misunderstand. I wanted to pass, but I wanted to stay with Auntie Muriel. Didn't happen, so Chepstow Road it was. I'd run to Aunty Muriel most weekends but holidays were difficult. I'd be dumped on Granny, who'd laugh at my voices and brag to the neighbours that I'd inherited her boy's talent for play-acting. 'Could have been a star, my Sidney,' she'd say wistfully, stroking the yellowed photograph on the mantel piece. I was always in the school play, living every character. They became friends I could bring home without an argument. I was better at being them than being me and…forgot the condition of my estate to rejoice in theirs. That's a sort of quote, Rosalind, another great actress, just as I liked it, but Mother didn't. When I got to Bristol, I had parts all the time. She didn't come to those plays either, but it was past mattering. I taught English in Maida Vale, had digs near the school. Home was a bus ride away but I never went. Not wanted, especially when Granny died and the money stopped.

Thinking of Mother sets my legs thrashing and I've been picking my scabs. They look terrible. She was mad, you see, but in those days no-one talked about mad, unless you murdered someone. 'Though this be madness,' I shout as Kebab Man slices meat from that twirly thing, 'yet there is method in it.' Kept herself tidy on the outside did my mother. No-one guessed, except Aunty Muriel.

I was the nuisance, squawking away like that blasted duck but all she did was turn up the radio and drown me out. A slap would have been better than indifference. She didn't have men, so I wasn't cramping her style. And how could I cramp; a skinny, slouch-shouldered teenager with a tatty hairstyle and a beaky nose, a nothing against her prettiness, however sour her face. She didn't even drink, but sat from morning till night staring through the kitchen window at the dog-beshitten garden, reading the newspaper, doing the crossword puzzle, smoking like a chimney.

She loved those bloody dogs, everyone a Bobby. When one died another arrived. She talked to them in *coochie-coo*; 'who's Mummy's diddledums, who wants pee-pee piddledums, who's a Bobby dazzler,' as she petted them, taught them tricks, let them in her bedroom, forbidden space to me, and wouldn't let me touch them. They hated me, learned that from her. I hadn't been home for years when she died but in I walked and there was a Bobby, teeth bared. So I booted it, upsetting Mrs Fuller next door who kept it until it bit her husband. She tried to foist it back, had the nerve to ask for the vet's fee when he did the mutt. I said 'you took it so you own it,' so I won't have a dog like other streeties, hate the bloody things, and I'm economical with string. That man Clark was economical with *actualité*, but he has a dog and can afford string and he doesn't know his French. The word is *verité*. Mistakes agitate me.

'Your mother was a self-obsessed neurotic,' Freddy's son, my nephew the doctor said, 'with a borderline psychopathic personality.' Mother passed borderline when she got out of nappies...couldn't stand me, couldn't stand anyone. He says the money from my father's family was her undoing. Otherwise she'd have had to get a job and get on with people. She thought the world owed her a living. Aunty Muriel said that. I earned a living, once.

It was the house that did it; thought it was hers. It was mine all along. Dad had put it into my name before Normandy. He wanted to set me safe; not free like now, but safe. She couldn't sell it and for that she hated me, driving me out, renting out the rooms, denying me its comfort like the mean dog in the manger that she was. Bitch in the manger, really, with the everlasting Bobby dog. 'Bitch, bitch, bitch bitch,' I scream, hitting the high notes and crow and cackle and clap my hands so loudly, Mr Ali warns me,

'Now Rosemary, keep piping down quiet, and you mustn't be doing dirty or Mr Haidar will stick in his nose and bring that social worker back.'

Need another cigarette. I hate to be put in, or put out, whatever. I remember her. She started off with 'we can find you somewhere safe,' 'I don't like safe,' I spat at her. Her lips were whispering 'pre-senile dementia'. That's the new definition for people like me. I may look out of it, but I keep up with the latest words. She was trying to be smiley-nice, but I had to stop her.

'Do I smell the stench of appeasement?' I bawled, scaring her with, 'frit frit frit'.

I'm a fan of Mrs Thatcher. Forced into retirement like me, though things had been getting on top. That parsley-chopping bastard brought her, the social worker not Mrs Thatcher, though daytimes I tuck myself away and shut the mouth. Shouting's for the night, to kill the silence. He says I do rude things when no-one's looking. Well he must be looking, though when Mrs Keep-me-safe asked what I did, he went red and pursed his lips. I don't do that often, just a little tickle and a scratch, but when I see him, I wave my arms and writhe about as if I'm…well you know what, but I'm not.

I blame the house. As the nephew says, a dose of economic reality would have done my mother good, got her out of that bubble. Bubble boom, bubble burst, the lady's not for turning, except I couldn't stay there…

Because it stank of her. She was everywhere, pattery-dog steps on stair treads following her, however much I shouted at her empty kitchen chair. I'd run to the Chepstow Arms, walk down Pembridge Road to Notting Hill, up Bark Place to Moscow Road and into Queensway, a few in the Redan or the Leinster then good old Westbourne Grove until my feet hurt and I reckoned I might sleep. Even Rosalind and Viola, who sang with me loud in the dead of night, could not dispel this havoc. 'Sell the house,' advised Aunty Muriel but 'my father had a daughter,' Viola said, wondering if Portia might be a better choice, or Kate, 'and he wanted me to live here,' I insisted. 'He wanted you to be happy,' Aunty Muriel said, 'and you're not.'

The school said a thorough rest is needed, and home I went; home, that place you come to when you have nothing better to do. And even then I couldn't, so they put me somewhere else. Where I'd have stayed, but Mrs Thatcher closed it, sent me to be cared for by the community but they couldn't because I had my house. 'Sleep there,' they said, 'and come for therapy every day.' I spent the nights in the back garden…never inside. She'd tap on the window, crook her finger, dare me to come in so I …gave the house to Freddy's boy. She'll keep away from him, knows he's got her measure.

Now she'll never find me. I'm off to Monmouth Road to listen to the birds, wrapping my blanket against the frost, doing my little businesses behind the garages like a sneaky cat. The chippy's watching, asking where I'm going, knowing I'll be back.

'I have,' I cackle, 'immortal longings in me,' and he laughs.

'It is five days since I am seeing her,' Mr Ali admits to Freddy's son, 'and I have searched the streets, all her usual places, even Monmouth Road.'

Doctor Crossley looks to Mr Ali for clarification.

'It is where she performs her necessaries,' Ramadan divulges with a blush, though this man is a doctor. 'And I have her money ready,' he adds, 'but she isn't coming and she isn't in your hospital. I have enquired.'

Freddy's son has already checked the other hospitals. Ibrahim Haidar crosses the road and, wiping his hands on his white overall, asks, 'why are you letting her roam the streets like a Bedouin? She wakes the dead of night with her yelling and throws empty beer tins at dogs. *Haram.*'

'Is every koftah on your skewer halal?' Ramadan shouts in irritation. 'We are looking for a missing aunty, so bugger dogs. We are worried because we are without her shouting. It is the silence which concerns us.'

Doctor Crossley is wondering if he shouldn't have had her committed, but she wasn't a danger, except to herself. He's begged her to come home so often, he knows the response before she utters it.

'It's her or me,' she says. 'I can't be under the same roof as that woman.'

He'll pass by the police station on his way home. Perhaps they've heard something.

Ramadan is frying two portions of haddock when the newsagent slips behind his counter and whispers, 'I think they've found her.' From the corner of his eye, he sees blue light stain the pale stucco of Monmouth Road and hears the distant howl of a siren. The fish is wrapped and handed over. He grabs his overcoat, scarf and hat, for it's cold, and follows the newsagent whose wife is left guarding their kiosk, her vermilion bindiya bright in the flickering strip light.

The commotion lures faces to windows. Dipping behind the houses, the unlit track to the ramshackle garages is slippery with ice. White-rimmed trees glitter in the light of the solitary streetlamp. A cat perches on a garden wall, its eyes gleaming with curiosity as Mr Ali, Mr Haidar and the newsagent edge into the lane. Ramadan sees an emaciated leg protruding from the stack of cardboard under the rubbish behind the builder's skip.

'It's her,' he says, recognising the ulcers black against a purple-mottled skin. Her socks are gathered round her ankles and her shoes are gone. A car draws up behind the waiting ambulance. Doctor Crossley accompanies the constable, bends forwards and nods. At a signal from the policeman, the ambulance attendants don protective gloves and bounce the trolley over the rough ground. One of them, a woman, grimaces at the sight and smell of Rosemary. Her clothes are hard with frost, 'like washing forgotten on a line,' murmurs the newsagent as her wizened body is lifted up. Before they cover her, Ramadan sees her expression is calm, softened by death.

'I do believe she's smiling,' he says.

'Why didn't Social Services do their job?' Mr Haidar asks indignantly. 'She is frozen to death. They pay good-for-nothings to stay home and eat free meals. Why not help her?'

'She never signed on,' Ramadan says. 'She didn't need the money and didn't like their questions. She slipped through their net like a little fish.'

When Doctor Crossley returns to his car, they pull off their hats in respect.

'We will see to her possessions once the police permit us and I must be giving you her credit cards and bank books…only right,' Ramadan says respectfully.

'You didn't know her before,' Freddy's son says sadly. 'She was such fun, especially when we were at school. English literature became a joy. There was no-one she couldn't bring to life. The first time I went to a theatre was with her. We saw Hamlet. I was ten years old and I still have the programme.' He pauses for a moment, realising they don't understand. But they looked out for her and deserve an explanation. 'Her mother treated her badly,' he continues. 'My grandmother, her aunt, died soon after her mother and Aunt Rosemary lost her bearings. The damage was too deep and her drinking didn't help.'

Ramadan nods. Though Allah forbids it, some of his friends have gone the same way, but their families do not let them push their affliction through the London streets. Rosemary wouldn't let anyone lock the door for her own good.

Doctor Crossley holds up a frayed book, its green cover stained with damp, its pages dirty. 'We kept her stuff in the garage and she'd collect a book from time to time, always returning it as if we were a library. Her face was resting on this. She must have died as she was reading it… Antony and Cleopatra would you believe.'

'There is writing on the page,' Ramadan observes, recognising the spidery script. 'Has she left a message?'

Doctor Crossley puts on his glasses, raises the book to the light and reads, "I'm not the clown, I'm the Queen, a dish for the Gods, my conclusion most infinite." He looks back at the rubbish behind which Rosemary died. 'Whatever that means, she's at peace. There'll be no more shouting.'

It's nearly midnight. As they walk along the deserted street, the silence is broken by a squall of fighting cats. The newsagent shudders. 'We believe that the soul enters another being at the moment of death and goes,' he says, 'to the place it loved the best.'

'I don't think our Rosemary is becoming a cat to howl on your doorstep,' Ramadan laughs. 'If she's anywhere, she's in the pub. But we'll miss her. It will be too quiet and we will listen for her voice.'

Ibrahim and the newsagent eye him with disbelief and shake their heads.

'Silence is when bad things happen,' he says. 'That's why Rosemary destroyed silence; to keep herself safe from what her mother did, when everyone kept silent. She shouted and no one listened.'

KRIK, KRIK, KRIK

The icy wind blustering along Portobello Road was breath-stopping. I was so desperate to be home, I was almost running but it halted me in my tracks.

'It' was a birdcage: a mahogany Taj Mahal with an intricately columned dome and carved spiral staircases below each of its four towers. A perch swung from the highest point and balance bars crossed transversely from the corners. Mirror panels inside reflected its perfection: the tiny ladder, intricate feeding trays and a miniature porcelain bath complete with brass shower pull. The cage trembled in the gusts, the perch swaying with an almost imperceptible 'krik, krik, krik'.

'Glorious, isn't it.'

I jumped. It was a Sunday morning in January. Portobello was deserted and I hadn't heard the man approach. 'Not that you'd keep a bird in it,' he said, jutting his chin towards the base. 'Shame to land droppings on that marble.'

I unlatched the cage door and touched the gravestone chill of the floor. The coloured frieze I'd thought painted was red and green cloisonné enamel and the inner balcony was floored with tiny parquet tiles. A drawer in the table-stand contained a miniature brush and shovel, their handles carved to match the columns, and some tiny scoops for seeds. Strings of multi-coloured glass beads dangled from the dome. 'Toys for bored birds,' I said. He laughed and unlocked the door to his shop. I followed him into the fusty unheated room and poked through bric-a-brac as he shifted battered portfolios to make space for the cage. Don't appear too keen, I told myself and waited for him to start the ball rolling.

'Cleared a house last week, a Social Services job; load of junk, bar that,' he said, lighting a cigarette and pointing through the grubby window at the cage. 'Lovely craftsmanship, nineteen thirties, definitely Indian. I took it home but yesterday the wife wanted it out, some tosh about the perch swinging on its own, and music. They get like that at a certain age.' His cigarette smoke curled into the dank air.

'Is it for sale?' I asked, keeping quiet about my living room window overlooking the dustbin store, not a pretty view, and I was sick of neighbours peeking through the window. The cage would block that, but I wasn't going to tell him.

'I'll sell you the shoes off my feet,' he chuckled, stubbing out his cigarette. 'Five hundred quid, delivery included.'

It was expensive. But, my inner voice whispered, it's better than keeping the blind down, and it's certainly a conversation piece. Suddenly a memory burst on me so unexpectedly, I shivered. The top floor of our old house had once been for servants and had barred windows. We didn't have servants, so us children slept up there. Daddy had always called it the birdcage. 'Stops you all flying away,' he'd teased.

I was the third of four girls. Jane was the eldest, Katherine two years younger. Nine years lay between me and Katherine. Megan arrived two years after me. By then, Jane and Katherine were at boarding school. Both had left by the time we went and were more like cousins, friendly but not close, and Megan…well, Megan. I stepped outside and ran my finger over the polished wood, feeling the dovetailed joints, imagining brightly coloured birds, sensing a tang of exotic spices, nutmeg, cardamom, saffron.

'Three hundred cash,' I offered. 'I'm local, in a lower ground floor, only a few stairs. It would save you lugging it into the shop.'

'Four twenty,' he replied.

'Three fifty,' I said. That provoked a loud suck through his teeth followed by a sigh of acceptance. He stretched his hand towards the birdcage as if bidding goodbye to an old friend. I pointed to the ATM on the corner and told him I'd be two minutes.

Megan flew before me. True to character, her departure was dramatic. She eloped in her first year at university with a married lecturer whose infuriated wife crippled him with alimony in revenge. Two years later Megan dumped him to find spiritual enlightenment on the hippy-dippy trail to Kathmandu, leaving her indignant lover a note accusing him of smothering her creativity with domesticity. But that was Megan, Daddy's favourite girl, who was forgiven everything. When she returned penniless, a dark-haired baby boy of undisclosed paternity on her tie-dyed hip and her eyes yellow with jaundice, he welcomed her home as Mummy watched sullenly. Ten months later, she and the boy went for a walk and never came back. We heard nothing for ages until a policeman arrived with a photograph of a body but no mention of a child. The post-mortem was predictable, the baby unfound despite extensive enquiries. My father was heartbroken, the words 'he'd be five now' on his dying lips. He'd be in his twenties now and we're none the wiser. Did he disappear into those outposts of society where no one cared about grand-parents? Or did Megan sell him for heroin?

The birdcage was beautiful. I polished the slender brass uprights of the inner cage and buffed the wood with beeswax. In a fit of whimsy, I placed tiny porcelain birds bought from the same dealer on the upper platforms, but when my elder sisters called round late one Saturday afternoon, they didn't share my reminiscences kindly. Their every activity had been scrutinised for propriety, appropriateness, that keeping-up-of-appearances which turned Daddy's birdcage into their prison.

'He'd mellowed by your time so you were spared the rows over what you could do,' Jane said, 'and he spoiled Megan rotten.'

'Because Mummy didn't like her,' I retorted, which they couldn't deny. My mother never cuddled Megan, wouldn't play itsy-bitsy spider with her and kept her literally at arm's length. Megan, bird-boned with tiny hands to our hearty Anglo-Saxonism, was like a changeling dropped onto us by an evil stork. 'I never wanted her,'

Mummy often said after yet another kerfuffle, and Daddy would shout, 'don't take it on the child.'

'Megan was a nightmare,' Katherine said, her bitterness unabated.

'It was Daddy's fault,' Jane declared, 'and Mummy wouldn't explain, even after he died.'

'Whatever possessed you to buy it?' Katherine asked.

'Impulse,' I replied and poured them a glass of wine before they left to collect their children from the Queensway ice rink.

When I was washing the glasses, I heard a noise and hurried to the living room. Jane had forgotten her scarf, I noticed, as my eyes went to the birdcage. The 'krik, krik, krik,' of the perch had stopped but a subtle movement remained. A faint aroma of vanilla hung in the air. Jane always wore sharper fragrances and Katherine, having taken her kids swimming that morning, had exuded an unmistakeable whiff of chlorine. I finished washing up and spread the dishcloths on the radiator before returning to the living room. The birdcage was still, the vanilla odour gone.

I'd promised my mother a new winter coat. We met at Marylebone Station and drove straight to

Harrods where the sale was still on. She found the Aquascutum she wanted though it needed alteration. I would collect it and bring it to the terraced house on the outskirts of High Wycombe to which she'd retreated after my father's death. Home had been a creamy double-fronted house with casement windows and a magnolia tree in Dawson Place. My parents had bought it on their return from India in 1948 after my father resigned his commission and entered the City, where he didn't do well. He left Mummy very little so our lovely house had to go. Yet, to this day I can see the relief on her face as she closed the door for the last time, handed the solicitor the keys and walked to the gate without a backward glance. When I asked why, her answer, 'I hated the place,' had shocked me.

My father wasn't cut out for a desk job, or life in London and with time, a cold melancholy had overtaken him. I was the product of a momentary thaw, a spark of reconciliation which died altogether upon Megan's arrival. Megan, I thought, as I drove to Bayswater Road through the park, winter's dead leaves turbulent in the stiff breeze, whirling as she had whirled to her sordid end. Mummy went into the living room ahead of me. When I came in, she was in front of the birdcage, her arms hanging limply at her sides.

'Isn't it lovely,' I said. 'I found it in Portobello. The dealer thinks it's Indian.'

For a moment, I thought she'd had a stroke. Her face was ashen as if she'd seen a hideous spectre, her jaw slack, her eyes wild. She sat down on the sofa. Uncomprehending, I crouched on the carpet before her.

'Make me a cup of tea, dear,' she said in a quivery voice. 'I had an early start, and I don't have the stamina anymore.'

It wasn't the reason, but I knew her too well to expect an explanation. Volunteering confidences wasn't her style. She detested the trend to public bean spilling, as she described it, preferring to keep personal matters private. I'd booked a restaurant off Westbourne Grove for lunch, but she shook her head, announcing she'd catch the two o'clock train.

'After three, the compartments are crowded,' she said by way of an excuse, 'and there might be no taxis at Wycombe. I hate the bus, full of screaming toddlers and push chairs.' She glared malevolently at the birdcage, rejected my every attempt to persuade her to stay and went to the car.

Ignoring my exasperation, she chattered all the way along Marylebone Road as if nothing had happened. Yet when we kissed goodbye at the station entrance, she announced out of the blue, 'I punished the wrong person. Megan shouldn't have been born, but that wasn't her fault,' and walked away without another word or, I realised afterwards, a backward glance.

I cancelled the table and went to see a French film at the Gate Cinema. *Les Indigènes* followed the lives of Algerian soldiers who'd fought for France in the Second World War yet were denied an army pension. To the French, those *anciens combattants coloniaux* remained undeserving, especially after Algeria's bitter struggle for independence in the early sixties. But Daddy had been the same, always banging on about India's ingratitude after everything the British had done. It was the only subject on which my parents agreed. Perhaps that's too simplistic a statement because Daddy loved India, whereas Mummy despised it.

'They simply weren't our equals,' she'd once remarked with alarming sincerity, 'and still aren't,' meeting the disbelieving stares of her daughters with equanimity. 'Not even those with English blood,' she'd continued, preening at the flush which tinted my father's face as he rose from his chair and left the room. Understanding that some long-suppressed contention had resurfaced, we'd squirmed in silence. Megan, less inhibited, had hurled accusations of prejudice, bigotry and whatever else came into her head at our unapologetic mother.

That night, I slipped into a deep sleep until woken by Benny Goodman's *Sing Sing Sing*, one of Daddy's particular favourites. At first, I thought the music came from elsewhere in the building and dozed off. Then I sat up abruptly. It was inside my flat and I could smell cigarette smoke. A peal of feminine laughter rang out. Terrified, I crept from the bedroom into the unlit hall. The front door was locked, the chain on. That laughter came again as the music faded. I edged into the living room, my heart pounding. In the light filtering through the blind, the shadow of the birdcage formed a fragmented scaffold across the floor. I switched on a table lamp. The room was empty.

A china parakeet was on the coffee table. I was sure it hadn't been there earlier, unless my mother had taken it out. A cake-sweet scent lingered, like Guerlain's Shalimar. I remembered the dealer's words, 'some tosh about the perch, and music' and began to shake. Had I bought a haunted birdcage? Did the ghosts of long-dead birds frolic the minute I put out the light? Were the former cage-owners still connected? He'd said it was from the thirties and Shalimar was the sensation of the age, as was big band swing. The idea was unnerving. I took a deep breath and marshalled my rattled wits. After all, the cage didn't squawk or emit foul smells, which it could have done. Instead it laughed, smoked and played Benny Goodman. I watched it carefully, wondering if it would treat me to some Glen Miller or Stephane Grappelli and then fell asleep on the sofa.

The telephone woke me the next morning. I muttered a fuzzy 'hello' and heard Katherine's voice shouting, 'what the hell happened yesterday? Mummy's raving about Megan and your bloody cage, and some woman called Myrna.'

'You'd better come over,' I replied. 'Something very strange happened last night.'

Jane and Katherine arrived together. 'It's not like you,' Katherine insisted. 'Even buying it was out of character, and you don't expect me to swallow this ludicrous story, do you?'

'Then explain Mummy's reaction,' I demanded. 'She mentioned Megan, not me, and who's Myrna?'

'Myrna used to stare through the gate in Dawson Place,' Jane said hesitantly. 'I overheard Daddy telling her it was better if she stayed away. Megan wasn't Mummy's baby,' she continued.

'There were no announcements, like when you were on the way and I was old enough to know.' She paused to make sure that I, in my addled state, understood that. 'Mummy brought you to our school sports just before Megan was born and she definitely wasn't pregnant.'

'So where did Megan come from,' Katherine asked, 'and why have you waited so long to tell us?'

'Megan was a touchy subject for everyone,' Jane said, 'so I shut up.'

Katherine was opening and closing the drawers under the cage. Her movements were distracted as if compensating for the void in her comprehension. She began picking at the base of one of them before pulling out the entire drawer. A photograph lay face down on the wood. She peeled it free and gasped. Daddy, in formal mess dress, was arm in arm with a very pretty dark-haired lady. The blur of time couldn't disguise the engagement ring sparkling on her finger, or their happiness as they faced the camera. Others were applauding and I could just make out my mother's parents, though they weren't smiling.

'That's Myrna,' Jane said, squinting at the picture under the light. 'I didn't know she'd been Daddy's fiancée.'

'I think we should go and see Mummy,' I said. 'It's time we found out what happened.'

'We'll ring first, in case she's at church,' Katherine advised, looking at her watch, 'and I must be back by five.'

'Myrna's father was a colonel in Skinner's Horse and based in Rawalpindi. Her parents sent her to school in England. War was declared. She left school and joined the Women's Royal Army Corps, but was posted "home" as she called India, to free up men for active service. I came to Bombay in '46 to join my parents,' my mother explained. 'They were great friends of your father's family. Everybody hoped we'd hit it off, but he wanted Myrna.' She grimaced at the photograph on the table before her. 'My mother had spotted something.' Her expression became censorious. 'You could always tell if there was a touch of the tar brush, even if they were fair-skinned.' Mummy realised that we were baffled. 'They had tiny hands,' she declared triumphantly.

Jane snatched up the picture. Mummy was right. Myrna's hand in Daddy's giant paw was like a child's, like Megan's.

'My mother discovered that Myrna was Anglo-Indian. That sort of thing was condoned up in 'Pindi. There was a confrontation. Marriage was impossible. Your father's parents were adamant. The wedding was cancelled. Myrna was made to return every single present, including the engagement ring. Your father bought her that blasted cage, and those stupid birds. They were the only things she kept. We married not long after and left for England just before Independence. Of course once Myrna's secret was out, she was ostracised. She returned to her parents. I heard they stayed on.'

'But I saw her here,' Jane sputtered.

'Her sort didn't fit anywhere,' Mummy snapped. 'The little bitch came here after partition and spoiled everything. Daddy was giving her money. That's why we never had any.' Her face warped with disgust. 'I caught them and for a while it stopped.' She looked at me resentfully. 'He blamed my mother, said she shouldn't have interfered. No-one had needed to know but she'd made sure they did, spreading stories, causing a scandal.' Mummy's eyes had a nasty glitter. 'I hated that half-caste tart,' she muttered, her face reddening with anger. 'He said she was a marvellous dancer and great fun.'

I felt sorry for my mother, even if I had no sympathy. She'd grabbed her chance, not caring whether the man she was marrying loved her, disregarding the possibility that he loved another, blamed Myrna for her inevitably unhappy marriage and their poor financial situation, though everyone knew my father was hopeless at business. I pushed for the truth.

'Megan,' I said.

'He admitted she was his but insisted I make up for ruining Myrna's life by taking Megan in. He promised he'd stop if I agreed, and he kept his word. Megan was given a family and legitimacy, but that was as far as I'd go.'

'Couldn't you have loved her simply as a child?' Jane asked. 'Lots of people who adopt manage that.'

My mother shook her head. 'The older she became, the more she resembled Myrna, the more he spoiled her. He even bought her Shalimar, Myrna's favourite perfume. If I were you,' she said, 'I'd burn that monstrosity. I won't set foot in your flat till it's out. It's how he found her,' she said, seeing my bewildered face. 'He saw it through a window and knew she had to be there. She'll destroy you the way she destroyed us.'

'Don't be melodramatic,' I moaned. 'Hypocrisy, prejudice, snobbishness; they did that, not the poor birdcage. It's a piece of wood and Myrna's dead, like Megan.'

She shrugged. The conversation was over. We left.

I propped the photograph against the cage when I got home. The scent of Shalimar didn't return, nor did the music. I'd occasionally hear the 'krik, krik, krik' of the perch when the draught moved it or in a vibration from the Underground which ran beneath the house. The cage was calm, perhaps because the truth was out, and I couldn't see why I should burn something so beautiful at the stake of my mother's resentment. But, 'poor Megan' I often whispered to it, 'punished for the mistakes of others.'

One night, I heard again that laughter and the laughter of a child. A woman was singing in an unknown language but when I entered the room, everything was quiet. I was about to leave for work the next morning when the phone rang. It was the dealer. 'The Social Services had assumed the old lady had no relatives, didn't check properly,' he said, 'and a son has turned up who wants his mother's things.' I suggested he send him round. 'He won't pay you a penny,' he warned.

When the bell rang the following evening, Jane, Katherine and I apprehensively opened to a gentleman a little older than Jane, accompanied by a young man called Mathew whom we guessed at once to be that dark-haired baby on Megan's hip before she disappeared for ever. They accepted a glass of wine and, as the story was told, everything fell into place.

Myrna had been pregnant when Daddy jilted her. The older man was our half-brother. After Independence, they'd travelled to England and Daddy, having discovered them, had supported his son as best he could but hadn't acknowledged him, or given him his name, nor had he played an active part in his life. Then Megan was born. Daddy wanted to raise her as his child and forced it through.

'Which was wrong,' the man said. 'He convinced my mother to give up the child she loved to a woman who hated that child for what she represented. By the time my mother realised, it was impossible to unravel without a lot of unpleasantness, though,' Daddy's features looked at us, 'it might have been better to bite the bullet and get it over with.'

'But she kept coming to our house,' Jane said. 'I saw her.'

He nodded. 'My mother really got involved when Megan returned from Nepal, stopped her in the street I believe. She brought Megan and the boy to me. I'm a doctor and was in Nottingham back then. We told Megan who she really was, but your half-sister,' he hesitated, 'my sister, was pretty far gone. I organised somewhere to live, and rehab, but she couldn't stick to it, would dump Mathew on us and disappear for days, even weeks. We only learned about her death because your father put it in *The Times*. We'd just had our second baby. It wasn't easy.'

'But why wasn't Mathew found?' Katherine was sceptical. 'There are records, health, social security. Megan wasn't fit for anything. She had to be on benefits.'

My sister's tone of voice was unpleasant but our new brother let it pass.

'She died in a drug squat in Bristol,' he explained. 'The only papers the police found showed her old address, your address and Mathew carried her name, your father's name, not ours. She'd brought him to England on a birth certificate issued in Nepal. He didn't have his own passport. He was a baby. Myrna called your father at his office. He told her to stay away from the funeral, said it would cause a stink. She was very hurt and held him and your mother responsible for what happened to Megan. When he asked, she denied any knowledge of a baby and cut all links with him. She was terrified he'd want

Mathew as he'd wanted Megan.' He took a sip of wine. 'We went every year to Pakistan when my grandparents were still alive. Sometimes Myrna stayed on, especially after Megan died. She had a godfather, a judge. He pulled strings, got us a birth certificate showing that Mathew was born in Rawalpindi with my wife as his mother. It was Myrna's idea and easier than going through an adoption rigmarole here, which might have involved your parents. Keeping them out of it had become an obsession. I'd already made blood tests to confirm the relationship between me, Myrna, Megan and Mathew, just in case anyone asked but no-one did. We moved to Dulwich, presented him as our son and that was that.'

Katherine was still dubious. 'Why weren't you found when Myrna died?' she asked.

'I should have spotted the signs,' he sighed. 'My mother was behaving erratically but refused to move in with us. She'd go on retreats for weeks, sometimes to an ashram, sometimes to a convent in Oxfordshire. God knows where she went other times. We didn't realise she'd destroyed all her personal papers, especially those about next of kin. The neighbours didn't know her, because she moved house so often and wouldn't let us visit as she was determined to keep Mathew's existence a secret though your father, our father, was long dead. When she collapsed in the street, she had nothing except a coin purse, not even a credit card. The authorities had no idea who she was or where she lived. The rent went unpaid so the landlord thought she'd done a flit and entered her flat but her things were still there. He called Social Services. Finally they identified her, told him he could clear the place as there were no relatives. But we'd started looking and…well…' His voice broke as he ran his hands over the glowing wood of the cage. 'This was all she had of the life she should have lived.'

'I can't believe that you, of all people, bought it,' Mathew said, looking directly at me.

'It came to me,' I replied, ignoring the incredulous stares of my sisters, 'and you must take it home, to where it wants to be.' I refused their offer of payment and agreed a time for the cage to be collected.

'You will visit us,' they said as we shook hands, knowing that we wouldn't.

Occasionally, I imagine the 'krik, krik, krik' of the perch. I'm sad I knew nothing about my father's other family until long after anything could be done. My mother avoids my house, says it stinks of Shalimar and accuses me of re-opening an old wound. That's rubbish, for that wound had never closed. I've kept the little porcelain birds, even though I no longer have a cage in which to put them. Sometimes I hear them singing.